Lifers

Also by Anthony Masters

LIFERS

Anthony Masters

Constable • London

First published in Great Britain 2001
by Constable, an imprint of Constable & Robinson Ltd
3 The Lanchesters, 162 Fulham Palace Road,
London, W6 9ER
www.constablerobinson.com

ISBN 1–84119–406–9

Printed and bound in Great Britain

A CIP catalogue record for this book is available from the
British Library

Chapter One

HM Prison Aston, South London
High Security A Wing
11 June 2001 – 2330 hours

Royston lay on his bed with the TV set flickering sound-lessly. Nothing was free-standing in his plastic Aston world. The table and chair had to be pulled out from the wall and opposite was the inadequate niche where he stacked his light reading, largely books by P. D. James and Ruth Rendell.

His entryphone bleeped and Royston grabbed at it, gazing down at his watch, anticipating yet another security search, all part of the new regime at Aston.

'Yes?'

'Time to check you out,' came the familiar voice on the entryphone.

'Now?'

'Why not?'

For some reason unpleasant smells lingered within the plastic walls of his pod, and as the soft footsteps came down the walkway Royston began to make a list. Lists were important to him. In fact he believed that compulsive listing was the one trait that might get him transferred from Aston A Wing into a less exacting environment, like a psychiatric hospital, or even Broad-moor, although Royston knew that he had competition from Rhodes over that.

He listed the contents of his cell every day as a rou-tine, but most of his lists were rather more academic.

5

They included birds of the British Isles, wild animals of North America, makes of cars, bicycles and trucks, insects, films, plays, countries, aircraft, ships and flowers. Recently, he had been running through the smells that hung on in his all-plastic environment – shit, vinegar, farts, body odour, margarine, feet, Marmite –

The shutter of Royston's plastic pod slid up.

'You don't normally pay me late-night visits.'

'This isn't a normal occasion.'

'No?'

'Stand up and face the wall.'

'Not going to bugger me, are you?'

'You should be so lucky.'

'My luck ran out,' admitted Royston.

'You're right there.'

Later, when his visitor had gone, Royston went to the toilet. As he sat there he began to make another list, this time of flowers of the hedgerow. After a while he went on to buggers he had known. Then Royston saw movement and half rose. But the blade of the knife was already slitting his throat and, in the last few moments of life available to him, he watched the blood splatter the plastic floor.

Lambeth Police Station
Undercover Briefing Section
20 June 2001 – 1100 hours

'Two killings in two days,' said Creighton. 'And in a brand new security unit. That's going some.'

Boyd, pleased to be filling an empty life again, had to agree. 'I see the media are having a field day. That's the last thing the prison service can do with right now. They don't need kicking when they're down, and they've been down for a long time – particularly at Aston.'

Creighton nodded. Boyd had noticed how his boss's

agitation had increased since they had both met in the spartan little room. Superintendent Creighton had a beaten look in his eyes. As a result, Boyd conjectured that a rush job was confronting him. He was relieved, for constant changes of identity were essential to his well-being, whatever the dangers. And he hadn't had an identity change for far too long. As a result, he had sat in his suburban home, defeated by memories and guilt, and drunk himself into the ground, surrounded as he was by photographs of his dead family.

'Considering the work that's gone into the unit, it's a disaster,' Creighton continued. 'The government are embarrassed and the CID seem to be at a loss. Do you want a scotch?'

'I'll have a juice – with plenty of ice.'

'Still off the booze then?'

'With difficulty.'

'The dry-out worked?' Creighton took out a bottle of whisky and a Britvic juice from the cabinet behind his desk, reminding Boyd of the early James Bond movies. Creighton filled two tumblers with ice. Shaken, not stirred, thought Boyd, deeply relieved to be back in harness.

'What do you want me to do?' he asked.

'Go into Aston as a new recruit.'

'A prison officer?'

'I don't see you starring in the lifer role. You wouldn't have enough room to manoeuvre – though, of course, you've done your fair share of professional elimination.'

The frozen silence deepened as Creighton realised he'd made an appalling gaffe. Two years ago, Boyd's entire family had been wiped out in a car crash. He had been the only survivor.

'I'm sorry.' Creighton looked down at the desk, studying the scuffed surface as if he was telling runes.

Boyd, however, had hardly winced. 'Don't worry,' he said reassuringly, almost compassionately. 'What *is* my role?'

7

Creighton was a heavy man, not fat, but big-boned, and the desk groaned alarmingly as he got up and perched uncomfortably on the edge, trying to be casual, trying to be laid-back enough to pass off his blunder, man-to-man, colleague-to-colleague. 'You're going in as a prison officer.'

'Who's in the know?'

'Only the governor.'

'Isn't he the radical flavour of the year – Neil Hathaway?'

'He's been reduced to a nasty taste in the mouth. But when he was first appointed Hathaway was very much the action man of prison reform. Aston was a tip. Old buildings, overcrowding. It wasn't nice.'

'So there's been a make-over,' said Boyd, sipping his heavily iced orange juice. He hadn't worked in months, latterly because of the dry-out. Now he felt like an empty husk, still screaming for a proper drink, but so far he hadn't yielded for when he was drunk he saw the family even more clearly. There was no oblivion.

'Aston's had more than a make-over,' continued Creighton. 'A Wing is state-of-the-art.'

'The satellite pod job?'

'Hathaway's own design.'

'And that got him the post of governor?'

'The poisoned chalice,' said Creighton. 'Of course he's experienced – been at Strangeways for ten years. I thought he was the right man for the job.' Creighton paused. 'But now I'm not so sure.'

'Explain these pods.'

'Didn't you see the diagram in the *Guardian*?' Creighton got off the desk and sat down in a battered leather armchair, signalling Boyd to take the other. 'It's a Dutch design.'

'The chairs?' asked Boyd, trying not to sit on a jaggedly exposed spring.

'A Wing,' said Creighton flatly.

'Impressive?'

8

'The system was built on the old rugby ground next door to Aston.'

'How many pods?'

'Six. More can be added, but they won't be now.'

'What about security?'

Creighton got up and began to prowl about the room restlessly, as if he had misremembered something and was feverishly looking at the scanty, scarred furniture and fittings in the hope that they would give him some kind of clue. 'The six pods are linked to a central satellite by walkways. A Wing is completely plastic in a sheath of steel, and beyond the pods is a high steel fence and beyond that there's another, even higher. A new security code is tapped into the computer every morning. So what went wrong? How in God's name were the throats of two inmates cut in two successive days? What are we looking for? Massive sleight of hand? Some murdering magician?'

'Where were the men found?'

'Sitting on the toilet.'

'What about cameras? Surely there shouldn't be any privacy? Aren't they watched while they defecate?'

'No. There are no cameras in the toilet. That was Hathaway's idea. Little bit of dignity.'

'That was damned stupid.'

'The inmates are searched half a dozen times every twenty-four hours. So are the pods.'

'Why didn't Hathaway get the message and put a camera in the toilets after the first killing?'

'He instigated more searches, but stuck to his privacy principle.'

'That was obviously a mistake,' said Boyd drily.

'OK, so Hathaway gave the men a little dignity, but there are cameras everywhere else in the pods. How could anyone have got to them? It's quite impossible.' Creighton paused. 'In the case of the second killing, the computer went down.'

'For how long?'

'About fifteen minutes.'

9

'So the cameras got closed down too?'

'Yes. Officers were sent to each pod as soon as the problem started, but the doctor says that the killing was almost certainly done before the problem with the computer began. I think it's a red herring.'

'So a pod is a cell with only one entrance. What are they like inside?'

'A circular space – spacious, with nothing that's free-standing. Rather like living in a bubble continuously viewed by CCTV cameras.'

'Except in the toilet area,' Boyd reminded him.

'A pod is a bubble you can't burst,' added Creighton.

'Obviously someone got inside at the crucial time,' said Boyd. 'Throat slit while shitting. Not much privacy after all. So how the hell did the killer get in?'

'That's the impossible question.' Creighton sat down again, looking defeated.

'So there were six lifers on A Wing?'

'Five. The sixth pod was never used. Now there are three.'

'What about staffing?'

'Sixteen in all, eight officers to each shift. Plus Ted Brand, the section head. The control room is in the satellite and each pod is watched twenty-four hours a day.'

'Is there anywhere else in the pods that the CCTV cameras don't cover?'

'No.'

'What's in the central satellite?'

'The association unit as well as the computerised control room.'

'How do the inmates get back into their pods?'

'There are hydraulic steel shutters that give access to plastic walkways.'

'Steel-encased too?'

'Yes. So when the lifers get banged up they stand in front of the shutter and an accompanying prison officer taps in an entry code which is different for each inmate

10

– and as I've already said is changed every day. Then each inmate's escorted down the walkway to his cell pod by a couple of officers.'

'Always?'

'Always. Then there's another security code tapped into the second shutter that gives access to the pod itself.'

'And that's also changed every day?'

'Yes.'

'Then what?'

'The pods are checked again and then it's time for bed. But despite all this, Jones's and Royston's throats were slit without anyone hearing or observing anything at all.'

'So it's an inside job.'

'How else could they have died?'

'The computer didn't go down both nights –'

'No.'

'CID got any theories?'

'Not yet. But the inside job is high on the agenda.'

'So what am I to do?'

'Do what you always do.'

'How do I get in?'

'You'll be an extra hand.'

'What about experience?'

'You've been in the Royal Engineers, only out a couple of months. A prison officer's job on A Wing is highly paid, but there aren't many applicants. Normally there'd be an internal transfer. But the job's becoming a little unpopular so an outsider can be an insider much more easily right now. We need to make an arrest. The Home Secretary's shitting bricks.'

'Could one of the other inmates be involved?'

'Anything's possible,' said Creighton.

'What about the officers on duty? What were they doing?'

'Watching the CCTVs. Checking the inmates.'

'All the time?'

'Most of the time. When a prisoner is under escort to

11

his cell, the other screws take a break from constant viewing. So there's a little bit of slack there – which has been tightened up.'

'Is Brand still in the job?'

'Yes.'

Boyd finished his orange juice. 'Tell me about the lifers.'

'Let's start with the dead. The first victim was Craig Royston, convicted in 1992 for murdering and disembowelling his wife and her mother.' Creighton paused. 'I know the feeling. The second was Aidan Jones who was convicted the same year for being a serial rapist who afterwards strangled his victims.'

'And what about the survivors?'

'There's Jon Jordan and Solly Parker. Jordan decapitated his girlfriend, and Parker went berserk in a park and killed five youths with a machete.'

'Don't these guys qualify for Broadmoor?'

'The jury considered Jordan sane – he killed because he got jilted. Parker was making a revenge attack on some louts who'd been gang-banging his missus. There again, the jury found him sane. And so we come to William Rhodes. His sister was raped and he killed her rapist. Then he got busy on other rapists, acquitted either for lack of evidence or some other technicality. Rhodes is a serial killers' serial killer.'

'Why didn't Hathaway split these inmates up after the murders? Disperse them?'

'He wants to find out what the fuck's going on. How security got breached, not once, but twice. And anyway, there's nowhere else to put them.'

'It's all a bit of a cock-up, isn't it?' Boyd was uneasy. There must be something everyone was missing. But then that's how most of these cases started. To an outsider the situation was inexplicable. To an insider who had worked his way into the infrastructure, a chink of light could lead to a clearer understanding. Becoming an insider, in Boyd's experience, was like a long dive into shadowy depths.

12

'If Hathaway loses his job it'll be a pity. He's a good egg.'

'How do you define a good egg?'

'Someone with professional competence who also happens to be a visionary – a rare combination. Hathaway has that combination.'

'Hasn't he just lost it?'

'I don't believe that. I don't *want* to believe that.'

'Maybe a prison officer was working with an inmate. Rhodes seems a likely contender. He's been the avenger on the outside, and now he could be doing the same job on the inside. But what beats me are these juries. Some of these men seem very disturbed. What are they doing in a maximum security wing at Aston? They should be in Broadmoor.'

'You wouldn't say that if you met them,' said Creighton.

'You've done that?'

Creighton nodded. 'Every one. They come across as regular guys. Except Rhodes. He's a little on the eccentric side as you'll no doubt discover.'

'So the current batch of inmates have become sitting ducks?'

'So is Hathaway.'

'Maybe we're limiting our options.'

'What do you mean?'

'Aston is a large institution and there's an awful lot of inmates and prison officers. Anyone could have had a slice of the action.'

'You may have to widen the net. But you've got to move fast. I don't want Hathaway to resign. No one does.'

'Because he's a good egg?'

'He's more than that. A Wing is his baby. From a lifer's point of view the pods provide a secure but bearable environment. "However disturbed the crimes of the inmates have been, however vile the violent crimes, if we're not to hang them, then we must at least

13

provide them with a productive life" – and I'm quoting that from Hathaway's book, *Humane Security.*'

'And do they have a productive life?'

'They're offered one – not all of them take it up.'

'I'd agree with Hathaway if I felt they were sane.'

'That's where you and the juries differ,' said Creighton drily.

'When do I start?'

'Tomorrow.'

Boyd gazed at Creighton as if *his* sanity was in doubt. 'What about building up my identity?'

'I'm afraid that's going to be on the hoof.'

'Who am I?'

'Luke Taylor.' Creighton took an envelope out of his pocket and gave it to Boyd. 'I'm sorry.'

'How do you expect me to digest all this?'

'You have your methods.'

'They usually stretch over a fortnight.'

'I'm afraid we haven't got time for that, Danny. You'll have to do what you can. This is an emergency. Don't forget, Hathaway's a good egg.'

Earls Court
20 June 2001 – 1400 hours

'You're going back in?' asked Marcia Williams as she and Boyd sat in a small private garden in a square just opposite her flat in Earls Court. He had yet to study – and then create – his new persona. But seeing Marcia was, for the first time, essential to his well-being. For Taylor, Boyd would burn the midnight oil.

They had been seeing each other since leaving Ravenscourt Park, the nursing home where they had both dried out. For many years Marcia had been in public and private partnership with Tod Lucas, making documentary films about African tribes, but Lucas had met another film maker – not in Africa, but in the more mundane surroundings of Hammersmith.

14

Marcia had not been able to cope with the shock and she and Boyd had hit the bottle at roughly the same time, ending up in Ravenscourt Park, in Boyd's case courtesy of the Metropolitan Police, and in Marcia's a medical insurance company.

Drawn to each other, they had outmanoeuvred a security system that was as tight as any prison and succeeded in sleeping together, alternating bedrooms with clandestine pleasure.

Because neither Daniel Boyd nor Marcia Williams had had sex for a very long time they had savoured the sensation, gradually realising that by some miracle each had found a kindred spirit, deriving additional adrenalin from beating the system.

Now, returning home, they had continued to see each other but, without the excitement of breaking the Ravenscourt rules, they were finding normality an obstacle.

Boyd was conscious that his own reticence was yet another drawback, for although he knew Marcia's personal history, he had not allowed her into his own private hell. All she knew was that he had been an undercover officer for the Metropolitan Police and had had a breakdown.

Mild sunlight stole over the trim grass and well-ordered flowerbeds and Boyd decided to even the score. He knew this was going to be difficult for the guilt was still like a painful growth, a cancer inside him, but he was determined to confide in her. Marcia deserved to know him better, had to see Danny Boyd, the real identity that had been slipping badly.

'I want to tell you something rather painful,' he said hesitantly.

'Are you trying to say we're past our shelf life?' She spoke light-heartedly, but looked abject with a sudden misery.

'I've got to go back to work.'

'Can you tell me about your job?'

'No.'

15

'When are you going?' She looked shut out.

'Tomorrow.'

'And is this the painful thing you have to tell me?' She took care not to look at him, concentrating instead on a young woman with a dog that was fouling the grass, almost directly underneath a sign which read DOG FOULING PROHIBITED.

'That's not on,' said Boyd. 'Shall I reprimand her?' He was anxious for an aggressive encounter as a diversion.

'In your official capacity?'

'I think not.' Boyd got up and approached the young woman. 'Your dog's soiled the grass.'

'Yes.' She gave him a basilisk stare.

'Could you scoop it up and put the stuff in the bin?'

'Scoop up dog shit? With my bare hands?'

'There's an old newspaper over there.'

'Do you normally approach perfect strangers and ask them to collect dog shit?' The young woman was half angry, half amused at his interference. 'Is that your neurosis?'

'I wouldn't say you were perfect. You shouldn't let your dog foul the grass. Haven't you seen the notice?'

'What notice?'

'Just behind you.'

She studied the words for what seemed, to Boyd, an unnecessarily long time.

Then she turned back to him. 'Why don't you fuck off?' she asked.

Boyd gave a little bow and returned to Marcia who was smiling.

'You haven't managed to see her off,' she said. 'The dog's fouling the grass again.'

'I'm afraid I have to report a mission failure.'

'Is that a first?' she asked.

'One of many,' replied Boyd.

When the young woman had strutted past them,

dragging her dog behind her, Marcia said, 'Do you ever feel completely out on a limb?'

Boyd smiled uneasily. 'Often.' He guessed she probably thought his wife had left him. But now the time had come for him to tell her the truth. Then he wondered if he was taking the risk only because he was going away.

'Did you ask to be given another job?'

'No.'

'Then what is it?' She was alarmed again. 'Are you married? Do you have a partner? Half a dozen kids? Grandchildren?'

'I had a family. I lost them.'

'Out of contact?'

'Permanently. I killed them.'

There was a long silence which Marcia seemed determined not to break.

'In a car accident,' Boyd added.

'Why didn't you tell me?'

'It was too big.'

'They're still with you?'

'All the time. But not so much at Ravenscourt. We seemed to be in a different world there.'

'A temporary life,' she said. 'Like one of your cases.'

She spoke with such understanding that Boyd weakened, needing to confide but realising that opening the floodgates could provide an excuse for a drink. Several drinks. Above all, he had to avoid that predictable loading.

'Do we still have a friendship?' she asked.

'Yes.'

'How long will you be on your job?'

'A few weeks.'

'Will you be in any danger?'

'I'm an undercover officer working for the Metropolitan Police,' he said. 'I assume different identities in different circumstances. The identities are healing – temporary – and dangerous.'

She said nothing, looking away towards a small pond in the middle of the garden on which a young boy was floating an exquisitely designed model yacht, sails filled by a darting wind.

'I've been living like this for the last couple of years. These temporary identities at least stop me from thinking about the past. For a while,' Boyd added after a long pause. Then he said, 'They were all killed at once. A clean sweep. Most of the time I wish I hadn't survived them.'

'When did you first go undercover?'

'After the accident.'

'What were you doing before?'

'I was a DI.'

'So being undercover . . .' Marcia paused. 'Means you don't have to make a new life of your own.'

'I'm grafted on to other people's worlds.'

'How long can you go on doing this?'

'I don't know. Going undercover's like alcohol. I'd been on the bottle for a long time before I ended up at Ravenscourt.'

'And you enjoyed undermining the regime. Even then.' She gave him a conspiratorial look and they both laughed, suddenly relaxing, some of the pain anaesthetised.

'What are *you* going to do?' he asked.

'I've been asked to write a column for the *Guardian*.'

'What about?'

'The travails of a dried-out dipsomaniac.'

'Are you serious?'

'Very. And then I'm going to write a book about Africa. A political book.'

'So you'll be busy.'

'I'm going to keep myself busy. Like you.'

Boyd got up – and then sat down again.

'Musical chairs?' she asked.

'I want to ask you something.'

'What?'

'Will you be going away? To Africa?'

18

'I'm not going anywhere. I've travelled enough. I have my notes and a contract with Macmillan. I want to stay in the flat and write the book, and there's the column to develop. I don't want travel to distract me.'

'Will we see each other again?' Boyd felt threatened by her unexpected self-containment.

'That's why I suggested you coming over here. To see if you would see me again and on what terms.'

'What terms do you want?' he asked.

'I thought you'd lay them down. You're the one who sets the boundaries.'

Why was she being so difficult? Boyd wondered. Or was she really not being difficult at all? 'They could be hard to stick to. Most boundaries are.'

'Particularly with alcohol.'

'Meaning the dry-out counted for nothing?' Boyd's voice was steady.

'Well, it was only an interlude for me,' she replied calmly.

'Do you drink – are you drinking again?'

'Are you?'

They both laughed again.

'I'm dry,' Boyd said after a while.

'So am I.'

'We could be lying to each other.'

'But we're not.' Marcia seemed confident. 'But if we keep to the same old patterns, then I'm sure one of us will start drinking again. It would be only natural, wouldn't it?'

'I don't think you *are* sticking to the same patterns. It's me who's doing that.'

'What else could you do?'

'Go back to being Mr Plod. I could even apply for promotion, or join another force in another part of the country. I could do any of those things – or none of them at all.'

'Or go undercover. Take a false identity again. How many times have you done it?'

'This will be the third.'

19

There was another silence, and suddenly Boyd wanted to make life less complicated for her.

'I don't enjoy what I have to do. But as I said before, going undercover stops me thinking. And there's always another possibility.'

'That you'll die?'

Boyd looked at Marcia in surprise. 'How did you know that?'

'I'm sorry –'

'No. I don't mind. But how did you know?'

'I can understand.'

Boyd shrugged. 'I like the possibility and I'm afraid of it too – I suppose.'

'You never grieved for your family – properly?'

'No.'

'Are they – buried somewhere?'

'In Sussex. In a graveyard at Burwash.'

'Have you been there recently?'

'No.' Boyd paused. 'I don't want to go alone. Will you come with me?' He was gabbling now, conscious of making a fool of himself.

'When?'

'How about now?'

She didn't hesitate. 'I'd like to do that. Have we got time?'

Boyd looked at his watch. 'We could be down there by late afternoon. I don't have to start this new job until tomorrow.'

Marcia got up. 'Shall we take my car?'

'Wouldn't it be –'

'I like driving,' she said firmly.

Marcia drove with a kind of cavalier pleasure, carving up other motorists, passing on the inside, and tailgating with headlights blazing.

After a while, Boyd, considerably shaken, said, 'I never realised you were so aggressive.'

'Am I?'

20

'Yes.'

'And I'm sitting next to a police officer. Might you arrest me?'

'I don't have anything to do with Traffic Division.'

'I just enjoy driving,' she said, passing a truck on a bend and speeding ahead, making other vehicles slow down. A fist was raised and horns blared. Then she pulled over on to the hard shoulder and brought her rather battered but tank-like Volvo to a stop.

'You drive,' she said.

'Have I offended you?'

'Not in the least, but I'm putting you under too much strain.' She laughed emptily. 'I thought you might wet yourself.'

'I never lose control.'

'Did you think I had?'

'You're a good driver – but you get yourself into some tight corners. Is that deliberate?'

'It's a bit like a game of chess. Not that I could ever play chess. I don't have that kind of patience. But like you – I think about death.'

'Do you need to take other people with you?'

Marcia shrugged but she didn't appear to be ashamed.

Boyd got out and walked round to the driver's door while Marcia shifted over to the passenger seat. He felt shaky, unequal to her.

'Would you take me here?' she asked.

'Sorry?'

'Fuck me.'

'On the hard shoulder?' Boyd gave an incredulous laugh. 'We could get into serious trouble doing that.' Now he was being absurdly pompous.

'Do you want to take a risk?' She pulled up her skirt.

'You're not wearing any knickers,' he said flatly.

'No.'

'This is a set-up.'

'Do you mind?' she asked.

'Have you done this before? Did you and –'

'No,' she said quickly. 'We never did.'

'Do motorways turn you on?'

'Fucking in cars does.'

'Meaning a small space is a challenge.'

'Meaning why don't you get on with it?'

Boyd decided that was exactly what he had to do.

'Excuse me.'

Boyd hurriedly pulled up his trousers. Ironically, what he had most feared was now about to happen as he turned to face the police officer who had parked his patrol car, hazard lights flashing, in front of Marcia's Volvo.

'I'm sorry. I was feeling exhausted.'

'No wonder, sir. You were using up a lot of energy.' His face was expressionless.

'Is it a crime to have sex?' Boyd decided a more direct approach might be preferable.

'It is on the hard shoulder, sir.' The police officer watched Marcia buttoning up her blouse. 'Do you have any means of identification?'

Boyd fumbled for his driving licence and Marcia did the same. The police officer took a long time studying them both until, with a sigh, he passed them back.

Boyd wondered if he should admit to who he was, but Marcia put a hand on his wrist, very lightly, as if guessing what he was thinking.

Then she spoke, quietly and guardedly. 'I'm very sorry, officer. We've only just met after a long time. What happened was spontaneous.'

'At least you pulled over.' He suddenly grinned at them and then looked embarrassed by his own spontaneity. 'But you aren't allowed to occupy the hard shoulder unless there's a breakdown or illness.'

Marcia nodded while Boyd decided to be as obsequious as possible. 'We're really sorry.' He paused, the easy lie coming to his lips. 'It's true we hadn't seen each other in a long time, and we forgot ourselves.'

The police officer brought out a notebook, studied the cover and then put it back in the front pocket of his uniform. 'I'm not going to book you – this time.'

'Thank you,' said Marcia. 'I'm grateful.'

'So am I,' said Boyd.

'See you don't abuse the hard shoulder again.'

A desire to laugh uncontrollably filled Boyd and he compressed his lips, unable to trust himself to speak.

Marcia chipped in again. 'I'll make absolutely sure we don't,' she said with an earnest fervour that only made Boyd want to laugh even more. 'Please accept our apologies.'

The police officer nodded and then abruptly returned to his car. It was not until he drove off that Boyd exploded into laughter, rocking to and fro. Then he remembered another drive and the grisly, unbelievable result and his hilarity abruptly disappeared.

As Boyd pushed open the wicket gate of Burwash churchyard he hesitated.

'I can't even remember where the grave is.'

'Why not?' Marcia sounded puzzled and he felt an impatience with her.

'I only came for the funeral.'

'Is there a headstone?'

'Oh yes. I had all that done – at arm's length.'

'Shall we go back to London?'

'No. I need to be with someone – with you.' His impatience had gone. He felt armed by Marcia's presence.

They walked down a broad path, a lush green valley below them, the sun briefly coming out from behind the clouds and then being swallowed up again, as if grey drapes had been drawn.

After a couple of false turns and having to retrace their steps, Boyd found the grave on a lower level that gently ran into overgrown grass and a small copse of trees.

They stood silently. There were wisps of dried flowers and a rusty model locomotive that had belonged to Rick. Marcia took Boyd's hand as she read the carved lettering on the headstone.

ABBIE, RICK AND MARY BOYD
MUCH MOURNED
REST IN PEACE

'What about the little engine?'

'Rick and I were into model railways and the layout's still in the attic. I haven't been up there again.' Boyd's voice broke and Marcia put her arms round him, resting her head against his chest.

Chapter Two

'Luke Taylor?'

Boyd got up, having spent over twenty minutes in a waiting room painted a vintage British Railway green. There was a table, plastic chairs and a dog-eared copy of *The Sunday Times* colour magazine.

'I'm Ted Brand.'

They shook hands. Brand was overweight and heavily jowled, with receding grey hair and a uniform that seemed stretched to breaking point. But his voice was deep and cultured – like the received English of a BBC newscaster of thirty years ago. His voice was his greatest asset, transforming bulk into authority.

'I'll take you over to A Wing right away.' He didn't waste words and Boyd was relieved. He'd only had a night to rehearse the persona of Luke Taylor, ex-Royal Engineer, divorced, now unattached, heterosexual and needing a job. There was an economic simplicity to Taylor's nature that Boyd liked.

Brand led him through a series of long corridors until they came outside into a concreted yard that was dominated by a twelve-foot steel fence with a steel shutter, guarded by a prison officer in a wire cage. There were CCTV cameras everywhere.

Boyd paused and looked back at the old Victorian buildings, dour and ugly, but brightened by a new roof

25

and window boxes full of geraniums, incongruous against the grey walls.

'There's been a total refurbishment of the cell blocks,' said Brand in his resonant voice. 'It's not as bad as it looks.' He signalled his colleague and the shutter slid up noiselessly to reveal yet another steel fence that was slightly lower. Again, a steel shutter slid up and Boyd was taken aback by what he saw.

'Quite a radical piece of architecture,' said Brand. 'The unit's been open just over a year and was functioning smoothly – until we ran into deep shit.'

The satellite building had six steel arms at the end of which were six steel pods.

'First of its kind,' said Brand. He paused. 'If you get the job, you have to remember how dangerous the inmates are, however normal they may seem on the surface. You must follow set security rules which have always been impregnable. Unfortunately, someone's managed to penetrate them. How they did that is anyone's guess – at the moment.'

'Do I have job security?' Boyd regretted the irony at once, but Brand didn't seem to notice.

'I'm afraid you don't. We could be closed down at any moment, particularly if the governor's forced to resign.'

'What do you think the chances are?'

'A fortune's been spent on this place, but I suppose the nonces could be held here.' Brand shrugged and then continued. 'There's nothing wrong with security. Someone's been manipulating the system – and I don't know how. None of us do.'

The next steel shutter slid up to reveal a small transit area with an officer behind a metal grille.

Brand passed through with a nod and then took out a key with a built-in laser beam, and yet another shutter slid open to reveal a circular space in which three prison officers gazed at three monitors that were fixed to a round stainless steel desk. On three of the monitors figures moved. The others were each focused on a pod which was empty, devoid of accessories.

Then Brand continued with his now familiar authority. 'This is the job from hell,' he said. 'After I've explained the system I'm sure you won't want to be a team player.'

Boyd said nothing, aware of the danger of sounding glib.

'Come and sit down.'

They sat together in front of a screen and keyboard while Brand tapped out a security code and three names appeared: Jon Jordan, Solly Parker, William Rhodes.

'There were five inmates and now there's only three – which is a pretty good record for a state-of-the-art top security unit, don't you think?' Brand gave a heartily uneasy laugh.

'How could security have been so badly breached?' asked Boyd.

'We all have the same level of clearance, and we're satisfied with yours, Luke, despite the fact you lack experience. Normally, we recruit from inside Aston, but even allowing for the high pay, A Wing isn't the place where prison officers want to work. Craig Royston and Aidan Jones were found with their throats cut, but I don't believe we're dealing with an inside job. I've a gut feeling the murders were carried out by William Rhodes.'

'How?'

'That's my problem.'

'He'd still need insider help, wouldn't he?' Boyd wondered if he was being too pushy by seizing the opportunity, but Brand showed no sign of unease. In fact his big fleshy face bore no expression at all.

'Not necessarily from this wing.'

'You're sure of that?' Boyd risked.

'There are over five hundred officers in the main prison.'

'But how could any of them be in touch with Rhodes?

27

It's not possible, is it, with all this high security in place?'

'He has concessions.'

'What sort of concessions?'

'Library books. He's allowed constant supplies for research. It's just possible a laser key could have been smuggled in.'

'Are these keys multi-purpose?'

'There's one type that is. Obviously we've had this checked out and the frequency's no longer compatible.'

'And that laser would open every door and shutter in the satellite, walkways and pods?'

'Yes. It was designed to be used in an emergency and overrides all other systems.'

'Isn't Rhodes watched by CCTV cameras twenty-four hours a day – just like the other inmates?'

'Yes.'

'So how could he have left his pod and got into Craig Royston's and Aidan Jones's – even with the overriding laser?'

'I wish I knew.'

'Why are you so unwilling to suspect prison officers in the satellite?'

'Because they're hand-picked.'

'I'm not,' said Boyd, wondering if he'd gone too far.

But clearly he hadn't, for Brand said, 'I have to say I'm impressed because I like the way you think. So I'm offering you the job.'

Boyd looked suitably gratified.

'But I have to tell you something rather important. No one else has applied for it.'

Boyd laughed. 'So much for the competition.'

'This is a rather unique situation. As I told you, the men in here are highly dangerous. The *most* dangerous. The whole ethos behind A Wing was the creation of an environment where these inmates are going to live for the rest of their natural lives.'

28

'Will they *ever* be released?'

'Not under any circumstances.'

'And they're sane?'

'Technically.'

'What does that mean?'

'It means they're volatile and given to violent mood swings.'

'Doesn't that qualify them for insanity?'

'Not necessarily.'

'How well do you think you know them?' asked Boyd.

'As well as I can.' Brand paused and then said, 'As you know, you'd be taking on a highly paid job. Did the money attract you?'

'I wouldn't say I had a vocation to become a prison officer.'

Brand nodded and seemed satisfied. 'OK. I'm going to tell you something about the inmates before you meet them. But tell me more about yourself first.'

'OK. I'm thirty-six, unattached and uncomplicated. I've spent all my life so far in the army – in the Royal Engineers – where I eventually became a sergeant. I've had postings in the Far East. For the last few years I've been in charge of a road-building project in Bosnia.'

'Why did you leave the army?' asked Brand.

'I wanted to lead a less structured life. But you'll still find me very good at self-discipline.'

'You had a glowing report from your regiment. That was what swayed me.'

'Thank you. You never know what they're going to say if you leave before retirement.'

'Are you married?'

'I was – to another soldier. Amanda Devnes. We split up last year.'

'You weren't getting on?'

'She went off with another bloke.'

'I'm sorry. Do you have children?'

29

'No.'

'A home?'

'I've got a rented flat in Surbiton.'

'That's not too far away.' Brand got up. 'Now how would you like to meet your new family?'

Chapter Three

Brand pointed the laser at the next steel shutter, which slid up to reveal another circular space that housed a snooker table, table tennis, darts and a mini-gym. There was also a wide screen television and a drinks machine.

The walls were a shiny plastic and gave off a slight glare. Concealed lighting made the glare worse.

'Plastic encased in steel,' said Brand. 'Not only escape proof, but the inmates would find difficulty in harming themselves.'

'Do they associate?'

'Rhodes doesn't.' Brand paused. 'I'll deal with the case histories as we go.' He aimed his laser key at a panel in the wall and a whole section slid back to expose another shiny plastic area, this time with a round table and six chairs, all welded to the floor.

'No kitchen?'

'Considered a security risk. The food comes from the main kitchens on a hot-plate trolley. We've got a good chef.'

'And they all eat together?'

'Occasionally. Most of the time they eat in their pods.'

'So this area's largely redundant.'

'We find that a problem. The governor wants to encourage communal eating – at least once a week.'

31

'What's he like?'

'I've always appreciated Hathaway. This is potentially the most effective lifer unit I've been on.'

'Except for the throats,' prompted Boyd.

'That's why Hathaway will have to resign. His head's on the block.' Brand sounded oddly dismissive, despite his apparent 'appreciation' of Hathaway.

There was a long silence until it became clear that Boyd was expected to further the conversation. 'So a prison officer's duty is to facilitate the smooth running of the unit. But what kind of relationship would I be expected to have with the prisoners?'

'You'll find they're mostly very withdrawn. They're all trying to create some kind of life for themselves. You must help with that.'

'In their plastic world.'

'Yes.' Brand seemed hesitant to express an opinion.

'Does the design get to you?'

'The place can be a real sweatbox in the summer, despite the air-conditioning. Let's move on.' Brand used his laser key on one of the now familiar steel shutters which slid up. Boyd saw another circular space which had a further six steel shutters, three to the left and three to the right of where they stood, marked 1 to 6. 'I'll show you an empty pod first. This one has never been used.'

Brand pointed the laser key at the sixth shutter which slowly rose to expose a long plastic corridor where the glare was at its worst. The walkway led in a straight line to another steel shutter that was about ten metres away.

Brand and Boyd strode on down the walkway, their footsteps unnaturally loud in the silence.

Then Brand opened the shutter. 'At last,' he said. 'The centre of a lifer's universe.'

The pod was large and reminded Boyd of a hotel room on a motorway services area where he'd once stayed in France. The place had been built in window-less plastic sections and Boyd had felt incredibly claustrophobic, waking with a dry mouth and a headache after a largely sleepless night because of the noise of the air-conditioning.

This pod was much larger, but there were still no windows, while wide seating ran round half the available space. Like the hotel room in France, the place was air-conditioned but it was quiet, obviously more high tech, with grilles which were too small for any kind of access.

'This seating converts into a bed by night. A foam mattress and blankets are supplied and are stowed away in this locker.' He pulled out a hatch in the wall. Then Brand turned to the other side of the pod, pulling out a table and a chair that locked into position. Above them was a shelf that could be used as a bookcase, below which was a built-in television set and video recorder.

'It's not uncomfortable,' said Boyd. 'Except the inmates have to face the fact that they'll live in this space for the rest of their lives. Maybe they'll even die in the pod.'

Boyd left the plastic world with considerable relief. To be in there for life was an appalling idea, whatever the surface comforts.

But how could two inmates have been murdered in these hermetically sealed pods?

'The more I see of this place,' said Boyd, 'the more mystified I am about the security breaches.'

'You're not the only one,' said Ted Brand drily.

Once back in the association area, Brand opened a shutter which led to a small exercise area that was surrounded by the lower inner steel fence and dominated by the higher outer one.

All that was possible to see was a sky that was grey and overcast.

'This is the worst part of the facility,' said Brand. 'The architect seems to have run out of ideas – or even space.

There was so much focus on the pods and their secure entries that outdoor facilities got overlooked.'

As Boyd stared up at the sky he felt much more claustrophobic than in the pod, despite the soft wind blowing on his face.

The steel sides of the satellite were two storeys high and there was barely a metre between the wall and the inner steel fence. Also, the fences were so closely meshed that virtually nothing could be seen through them.

All the inmate could do was walk along this narrow asphalt strip, and all he could see of freedom was the sky, grey and daunting as it was today.

'Of course,' said Ted Brand, noticing Boyd's unease, 'the sky is ever-changing.'

The space was almost too narrow for his bulk, but Boyd could walk up and down, counting his paces, staring up until he nearly bumped into the steel fence. He turned abruptly, strode back towards Brand and came to a stop.

'Do the inmates come out here much?'

'Only Rhodes. He's out here for hours. Would you like a break and some coffee? I could run over the case histories, and then we can pay the inmates a visit.'

But Boyd didn't move. He had never felt so trapped in his life and the very thought of any human being making this short walk, maybe dozens of times a day, knowing he would never experience anything else, was appalling, no matter what crime he'd committed.

'I can see you're badly affected by this.'

'I can cope,' said Boyd hurriedly, cursing himself for betraying his feelings.

'Don't worry,' Brand replied. 'I felt the same. Always feel the same.'

'Why couldn't the architect have given them a little more room?'

'One of my campaigns is to get an exercise area built on the other side of the satellite. There's waste ground earmarked for the expansion of the main prison, but

I don't see why we couldn't demand a bit of extra space.'

'Why did Hathaway agree to this?'

'I don't know.'

'He's been here himself?'

'Of course. He approved all the plans. In fact he designed the place. As I said, the architect was only a lackey.'

'So *why*?'

'I don't know. I've made the point and for some reason he's ignored it. Can I call you Luke?'

'Please do.'

'We're all on first name terms here. I'm Ted.'

Boyd looked back at the narrow space between the wall and the inner steel fence and shuddered.

Over coffee in the surveillance area, Brand introduced Boyd to another prison officer who must have been in his fifties and was tall and slim, with a shock of dark hair.

'Bill Farley – this is Luke Taylor. I was going to put you two together. Bill's one of the most experienced and long-serving officers at Aston.'

'That didn't help me when I came in here.' Farley had a slight accent which Boyd tried to place. Could it be West Country? Or Forest of Dean?

Boyd stirred sugar into his black coffee and wondered what kind of impression he'd made so far. Had he asked too many questions? Had he deferred sufficiently to Brand?

The trouble was that he couldn't get Marcia out of his head. A week ago they'd been manipulating the security at Ravenscourt, and now she was making freedom so attractive that he was determined to pack up this damned undercover work which he'd originally needed so much and was now finding such a trap. If he went back to being a DI and tried to get promotion, he and Marcia could spend much more time together and maybe, just maybe there'd be a future. The idea rather shook him, for Boyd had never even considered such an idea.

'Bill's our fount of wisdom about the inmates,' said Brand. 'He gets on with them better than anyone else and of course he's in their confidence.' Brand grinned, and Boyd wondered if he was winding him up.

'Shouldn't think they'll have much confidence in me now,' said Farley. 'Those poor sods got their throats cut in a top security unit. Once is dreadful, but twice is a massacre.'

'We haven't got any leads,' said Brand irritably. 'And because of that I reckon we'll be closed.'

Not while I'm about, thought Boyd, for he knew that his presence would prevent at least immediate closure. But for how long?

'What about Rhodes?'

Bill Farley laughed derisively. 'He couldn't have got the opportunities. He just couldn't.' He glanced across the table at Ted Brand. 'You tell me how he could have got access.'

Brand contented himself with a shrug.

Boyd had the sudden feeling that Farley and Brand didn't get on. He wondered how deep that went.

'There's a plot,' said Farley. 'And it's thickening. So call me paranoid.'

'If there's a competition for being paranoid I'd win hands down after this lot. You seen the *Mail*?' Brand got up and rummaged in a basket. 'I threw this away this morning, but you might as well have a look at what we're up against.'

STILL NO ARREST IN PRISON MURDER MYSTERY
Eight days have passed since the second murder in A Wing at HM Aston Prison. No arrests have been made since two life-serving prisoners, Aidan Jones and Craig Royston, were found on the toilet with their throats cut.

Neil Hathaway, governor of Aston, had this to say:

'The CID are conducting their investigation both inside and outside Aston. We believe these are revenge killings. All prisoners serving life sentences for violent crimes are being held in A Wing – our new security satellite – and we cannot ascertain how security has been broken, not once but twice.'

The satellite was opened by the Home Secretary just over a year ago and has been considered a model environment with good, secure conditions for five men who have committed such violent crimes that a life sentence for once really means life imprisonment.

Unofficial police sources also believe that the killings could have been 'executions', and are investigating the backgrounds of staff and prisoners alike in both the main prison and A Wing itself.

In addition, all prison officers on the satellite are now under surveillance, as well as the three remaining prisoners in Pods 3, 4 and 5.

One of the three surviving inmates is William Rhodes, who killed his sister's rapist and then embarked on a moral crusade, murdering other suspected rapists. When sentenced six years ago to life at Leeds County Court, Rhodes entered a plea of insanity, but the jury didn't accept his attempted mitigation and sentenced him to life imprisonment.

Rhodes was transferred to the Aston A Wing some months ago.

Boyd put down the *Mail*. 'So Rhodes is the new kid on the block?'

Brand turned to Farley. 'I was going to introduce Luke to the remaining three lifers, but why don't you do the honours?'

'I don't want to interfere,' Farley began.

'You're not,' said Brand. 'You're relieving me of one of my responsibilities.' He turned back to Boyd. 'The point is that Bill relates to the inmates far better than anyone else on the staff, and that includes me. I think you'd get more of an insight into these guys if Bill took you under his wing while you work your way in.' Brand paused. 'Bill's got a lot of perception. I wouldn't mind betting he'll be the one to crack the security problem and tell us how the killings were done. Unless he did them himself, of course.' Brand laughed.

Farley frowned and then grinned, as if he was forcing himself to join in a joke that was in rather poor taste – which of course it was, thought Boyd.

What's Brand like to work with?' asked Boyd when they were alone, determined to catch Farley while he was still unsettled.

'He's good,' said Farley. 'Gives me a lot of back-up.'

Boyd realised he had asked the question too soon and cursed his misjudgement.

'I heard you were in the army,' continued Farley as they walked slowly up the plastic walkway.

'Royal Engineers.'

'Just out?'

'Couple of months ago.'

'This job's all right,' said Farley. 'But we don't get any new recruits. That's not been a problem so far, though. Officers tend to stay in the job here because of the high salary.'

'You enjoy the work?'

'I wouldn't say that. I'm an ex-army man myself – SAS. I softened up, didn't I?' Farley laughed and Boyd felt relieved. 'Anyway, I've been out of it for twenty years. I can't say I enjoy prison life, but the inmates can be surprising.'

'How do you mean?'

'These lifers, they've done terrible things, but they're as normal as you and I.'

'How do you make that out?'

'Banged up here they're on the defensive, but once you get past that – they're normal. As I say, they're just like you and me, except they went that bit further – and once they'd gone that far they carried on.' Farley paused

38

and then said, 'I often think they overstepped this boundary which the majority of us accept. How many times have you said, "I'd love to kill her" or "I'd love to kill him" without the slightest expectation of doing it? Well, they went and did it, so the next time killing was easier. They did some appalling things in overstepping those boundaries, but when they got back again they were just like you or me. I guess that's why I get on with them. I'm a normal sort of chap – and I can recognise another normal sort of chap. The trouble is, most of the prison staff think the inmates are all animals and don't relate to them. They don't even try.'

'How do *you* think these inmates were murdered?'

'It's an inside job, isn't it? I reckon it was someone on the staff. Warped like. Got a kind of moral crusade.'

Boyd was suddenly much more alert. 'You really believe that, do you?'

'It's a hunch, that's all.'

Boyd didn't want to push him any further.

'And I'll tell you something else,' said Farley. 'The remaining inmates are shit scared. They think someone's out to knock them off, one by one. Except Rhodes of course. He's too preoccupied.'

'He's a moral crusader, isn't he?'

'Maybe he is,' agreed Farley rather grudgingly. 'But there's no *way* Rhodes could have killed them. It just wouldn't be possible.'

'Is he a normal chap as well?'

'That's the way I treat him.' Bill Farley cleared his throat impatiently. 'Just like I do the others.'

Farley knocked on the door of the pod, pointed his laser at the lock and the shutter slid up to reveal an extraordinary sight. Hundreds of books were stacked against the plastic walls, and were spewing all over the floor, surrounding a small desk and a chair behind which sat a tall, rangy man, dressed in blue trousers and a shirt, a pipe clenched in his teeth. He looked exactly like the stereotype of a rather dishevelled prep school master, with a long, narrow face, black beard and moustache, and a tangle of tousled black hair, uncombed but swept back from a heavily lined forehead.

'This is Mr Rhodes,' said Bill Farley. 'I've brought along a new member of staff, Luke Taylor, to meet you, William. He'll be working with me for a while.'

Rhodes nodded and his gaze returned to the desk where he seemed to be preparing some kind of manuscript.

'William is usually very busy in the day,' said Farley. 'He's writing a history of the English-speaking peoples.'

'I thought Churchill had done that,' said Boyd, and then wished he hadn't made the careless and involuntary statement as Rhodes turned to stare at him, taking his pipe out of his mouth and placing it carefully in an ashtray that was piled high with spent tobacco. The pod smelt of St Bruno.

'Exactly,' said Rhodes. His voice was quiet and cultured. 'But I thought I could be more comprehensive.'

Boyd took a grip on himself. Rhodes's activity had come as a shock. The moral crusader was buried in history. 'It sounds fascinating,' he said in a more considered tone, conscious that Farley was growing tense. 'Where are you starting?'

Rhodes picked up his pipe again and replied courteously. 'Where Churchill began – where we all have to begin. In the summer of the Roman year 699.' Rhodes lit his pipe. 'It's a project I've always wanted to embark on, but I've never had the time, never had a hope of having the time. But I've got that now and I'm forty-six and in pretty good health. In fact, as I shall be spending the rest of my life here, I'm allowed as many books as I want.' Rhodes leant back. 'I never married. I never had any responsibility to anyone – except to my sister, of course, which I managed to fulfil before I came here. What better way of spending the rest of my life? I've got my books, a good supply of paper – and my research assis-

40

tant, Mr Farley. My only regret is that I can't actually go to the London Library in person, but I subscribe and they send me the books I need. Mr Farley goes to the lending libraries. Of course, they're sadly under-stocked, but I have to say that he is a diligent researcher. What would you do for the rest of your life if you were given the choice, Mr Taylor?' Rhodes asked with sudden and surprising interest.

Boyd was seriously stuck for an answer and quickly changed the subject. 'What did you do in civvy street?' he asked, conscious of taking the wrong tone, of not being able to meet this bizarre man even half-way.

But Rhodes answered courteously enough. 'I was a lecturer in history at a polytechnic which now calls itself a university but is still only a polytechnic.' He chuckled appreciatively while Boyd tried a more leading question.

'Do you intend to submit your manuscript for publication?'

'Good God, no.'

'But the work –'

'The work is my life, Mr Taylor. I don't want it to end before I do. If that takes place, I'll be in despair and looking for a way out. Committing suicide is extremely challenging in this environment, so I just have to hope my work lasts me. While I have the London Library and Mr Farley, I can keep it going indefinitely.'

'Don't forget I'm retiring in five years' time,' said Bill Farley, breaking into Rhodes's monologue.

'Then I'll have to get myself another researcher. You're a young man, Mr Taylor. How would you like to take on the mantle?'

'I may not be here that long.'

'Faint-hearted, eh? And how do you regard history? As a conspiracy?'

'Not at all. I've read and admired Churchill's great work and if you're going to be even more detailed I'll be most interested. I'd like to read what you've written so far.'

'I'm afraid I don't allow anyone to see my work.'

'Not even Mr Farley?'

'Not even Mr Farley.'

'Are you nervous of people's reactions?'

'Not at all. But I don't need advice as much as I don't need publication. I want to read and write. That's all. Does that sound pathetically unambitious to you, Mr Taylor?'

'No.'

'I'm delighted to hear that. Now – if you'll excuse me – I must get on. And, by the way, Bill – could you return the Mullins book and try to get me Volume II? I'd be grateful if you could do that as soon as possible.'

'I'll go this afternoon.'

Rhodes raised a hand in thanks and dismissal, but Farley said, 'Are you getting nervous?'

'If you mean am I made nervous by what has been happening here, my answer is no. I don't recognise the real world. I find the place far too sordid. And now, if you wouldn't mind, I have a book to write.'

'He seems content,' said Boyd. 'Or am I being naive?'

'There's a force that drives him,' answered Farley enigmatically. 'And he's a very dangerous man. But he's set himself a life task and I'm willing to play my part. As you can see, he has no sense of personal gain or vanity. The task is there to distract him. Permanently.'

'So he's single-minded.'

'To the point of unnatural obsession. The rape and murder of his sister, Tabitha, pushed him into such tunnel vision that he found her attacker much faster than the police. He cut him up into little pieces and disposed of them in the Wey Navigation Canal.'

'And then?'

'He relentlessly located another four alleged rapists, cut them up and disposed of them in a number of different rivers. Water, the great purifier.'

'When was he arrested?'

'About six years ago. He's been in a variety of different units, including Aston, but I think A Wing is where he's at his happiest – and most productive.'

'Why wasn't he declared insane?'

'Because I don't think he is.'

'But that relentless pursuit –'

'That was simply the action of a single-minded man who was very angry. He and his sister had always lived together and they meant everything to each other.'

'And not content with avenging her, he was so consumed with rage that he went after another four rapists and cut them up too. My God, how did the court manage to find him sane?' Boyd was genuinely concerned.

'Because he *is* sane,' Farley insisted. 'He's just very focused. His mind is tidy even if his surroundings aren't.'

'Could he have had something to do with Jones's and Royston's murders?'

'I'm sure he didn't. The book is his all-absorbing interest now, not the pursuit of rapists. Believe me, I know him.'

'Just from being here?'

'No. I came from Strangeways. William was there for a while and then we both came to Aston. I've been close to him for several years now and had to observe the strictest security. Every book, every piece of research I get him, is strictly vetted.'

'Wouldn't he find his researches easier if he could go on the Internet?'

'That's one outlet that's not allowed here. Imagine Rhodes in a chat room.'

'How long has he had you as his research assistant?'

'That's been a gradual process, and an assumption on his part.'

'And he swapped chopping up rapists for a history of the English-speaking peoples – just like that?'

'It's all a question of availability. He had a natural

43

pause for his prosecution. But he read history through-out the trial and never even looked up.'

'Jones was a rapist.'

'I'm sure that William has only one thing on his mind nowadays. The book.'

'Yes,' said Boyd, trying to conceal his impatience. 'I think you're probably right. But how do you explain the killings? Do you really think they could have been carried out by a member of staff?'

'That's only one theory. The operation was highly organised. Two men were executed. Their crimes were very different and they had no personal connection with each other. So why? I've racked my brains and so has Ted Brand. So has everyone who works here.'

'You've not got any other ideas?'

'None at all. At least . . .'

'What?'

'This is a brand new project, still at the experimental stage. The question is, can a man be punished and yet be productive? Well, that's the policy here and I believe in that policy. But suppose someone didn't and wanted to close the unit down? Or maybe had a grudge against Neil Hathaway and didn't want him to succeed?'

'Does Hathaway have enemies? The sort that would really go to these lengths?'

'I'm sure Hathaway has enemies. If he goes, this unit will close.'

Boyd nodded, not wanting to push Farley any further. He'd been useful, but he didn't want to appear too curious. 'What's next?' he asked.

'Lunch. We'll do Jordan and Parker this afternoon. You won't find them as interesting as Rhodes.'

'You admire him in a way, don't you? I mean, for the book, not the killings,' Boyd corrected himself hurriedly.

'I don't exactly admire him, but I have to tell you he fascinates me. Doesn't he fascinate you?'

Boyd admitted that he did.

44

Chapter Four

Boyd and Farley walked over to the main part of the prison for lunch and queued up in the canteen. The more he got to know Farley, the more impressed Boyd was with his perception. The fact that he believed in the wing but also understood the flaws seemed remarkably objective.

When they were sitting down at a table with fish and chips for Boyd and lamb casserole for Farley, Boyd began to gently sound him out on Neil Hathaway.

'He'll want to see you over the next few days,' said Farley. 'He sees all new staff personally.'

'How do you rate him?'

'He's a bit of an idealist and doesn't always back up his ideas with enough hard facts, but the Home Office originally saw him as the saviour of the British prison system – especially here at Aston. And I don't just mean the new unit either.'

'That's quite a reputation.'

'Aston was filthy, a disaster waiting to happen a few years ago. But Hathaway completely refurbished the main block and conditions are much better for inmates and staff alike. Then of course there's the satellite and its lifers. There's also been an excessive amount of unwanted media attention – which highlights the current disaster.' Farley paused. 'We're just about coping.'

'What about extra security?'

'Everything's been tightened up. We don't let them out of our sights now.'

'Except whilst on the toilet.'

'Brand's put an officer on each of the shutters now. *No one* could possible get in.'

Boyd hurriedly changed the subject. 'Will Hathaway resign?'

'Only if he's pushed.'

'Who'll do the pushing?'

'The Home Office. Duncan Bryant is the minister concerned.'

'So it's all over for Hathaway . . .'

'I would have thought so – unless he can find a solution.'

Boyd decided to stop asking questions and for a few moments they ate in silence until Farley took the initiative. 'Married?'

'Divorced. You?'

'I'm divorced. I suppose I'm now wedded to the job.' He paused. 'And it's antisocial – like any shift work.' He dug in his pocket and brought out a printed card. 'This is your schedule and starts from tomorrow. I think you'll find your job description fairly onerous.'

Boyd scanned the card. 'Will you be around?' he asked hopefully.

'My own schedule has been rearranged so I can look after you.'

'Brand's instructions?'

'Yes. I can't repeat to you enough that these men are dangerous and you have to get to know their ways. You mustn't give in to them.'

Boyd read the card more carefully.

The prison officer is expected to:

1. Maintain secure custody in a context where people are held in confinement against their will.
2. Provide prisoners with humane care.

3. Provide prisoners with opportunities to address their offending behaviour.
4. Assist with day-to-day management in the complex organisational environment of the prison.
5. In the case of Category A prisoners, more individual approaches are necessary.
6. Prison service psychologically supports the prison service statement of purpose and staff by applying sound psychological principles and highly professional standards to the delivery of agreed organisational objectives; the understanding of individuals; the design of strategies for change; and the evaluation of effectiveness.
7. Prisoners (and their visitors) are to be hand searched and electronically scanned daily to identify drugs, weapons and explosives. Secure special units accommodate some of the most dangerous prisoners in the prison system.

Your daily schedule is as follows:
0730 Roll check
0800 Breakfast served to the inmates in their pods
0900 Activities that will include education and work
0945 Check for evidence of unauthorised activities and illegal substances
1000 Supervision of exercise
1100 Pod searches
1130 Paperwork to be completed, including:
　　　 – Complex sentence planning documents
　　　 – Observation books
　　　 – Suicide watch logs
　　　 – Individual history sheets
1230 Lunch, either in pods or communally in association area
1330 Paperwork as above
1400 Supervision of exercise (2 hours) (Can be outside or in association area)

1600 Tea
1700 All inmates are allowed out of their pods to watch television in association area, socialise with others, play pool, table tennis, table football (2 hours)
1900 Dinner, either in pods or communally in association area
2000 Lock-up

'Well?' asked Farley.

'As you say – onerous,' said Boyd.

'And that doesn't include our new duties.'

A bell shrilled and they both got to their feet. 'We don't have to go and see Jordan and Parker in their pods,' said Farley. 'They're a little more convivial than Rhodes, so they're usually having a game of pool after lunch.'

'Do they get on?'

'They've been the least trouble.'

As Boyd and Farley strolled into the reception area, one of the other prison officers said, 'Luke Taylor? You're to see the governor at 1600 hours.'

'Lucky you,' said Farley. 'He doesn't usually make appointments to see new staff so quickly.' He pointed his laser at the steel shutter which rose, admitting them to the association area where two men were playing pool. One of them was short and fat, clean shaven with ginger hair, while the other was tall, almost emaciated, with a small, bald head and parchment-like pallor. 'We call them Tweedledum and Tweedledee,' whispered Farley. 'On the left of the pool table we have Mr Jon Jordan and on the right we have Mr Solly Parker.'

'Fuck off,' said Parker equably.

Jordan said nothing, gazing intently down at his cue. He played his shot and then turned to Farley and Boyd. 'Extra staff, Bill?'

'Just one.'

'That all they can afford?' He spoke with a middle-class accent, while Solly Parker contented himself by saying. 'Fucking useless,' in a far less cultured tone. Then he, too, turned to Boyd. 'What kind of wanker are you?'

'The best kind.' Boyd tried to be witty and failed. No one even raised a smile, including Farley. From past experience, Boyd realised he was about to be put on test and felt suddenly drained of energy.

'You here to protect us?'

Boyd decided not to reply.

'You turned up to stop us getting our throats cut?'

'I'm here to see you're supervised,' said Boyd carefully.

'You mean, while our throats are cut?' continued Parker, his face expressionless as he turned to Farley. 'Or does this one want to get up my arse?'

'Come on,' said Farley mildly. 'You need to speak nicely to the gentleman. He's only learning the ropes.'

'Bit of sado-masochism then?' Parker continued his crude bantering. 'That should keep us going for a bit. You don't look as if you can handle yourself, let alone protect us. And we need protection, don't we, Jon?'

'You're right.' Jordan spoke slowly and with conviction. 'But I'm ready to fight for my life. Maybe you'll help me?'

'Of course,' replied Boyd. 'Who do you think killed those inmates?'

'We're spoilt for choice,' said Jordan. 'The Mafia, the management, right-wing lobby or an inmate.'

'Or maybe the whole fucking lot,' suggested Parker, positioning his cue and playing a clumsy shot. 'Shit!' He walked away from the table, cue outstretched, heading for Boyd. 'You want to prove yourself?'

'How?'

'Take me on?'

'No way.'

'Scared?'

'You're like a kid.' Boyd was determined to put him in

49

his place, conscious of Farley watching him. There were no other prison officers in the association area. So this *was* time for the test.

'I asked you to take me on.'

'And I told you I wouldn't. I'm not afraid of you.' Boyd spoke slowly and deliberately. 'Got it?' Why was Farley allowing this situation to slide out of control?

He stood still, knowing he had to wait until Parker made a move.

Suddenly his long, lean body tensed and he threw his cue on the floor. 'Come on then.'

'Where?' Boyd's tone was ironic.

'All right, Parker. Leave it.' Farley was remonstrating with him at last, but now Boyd wished he hadn't intervened. He had to prove himself and some of his energy returned.

Parker was still heading towards him, eyes fixed on Boyd, a little smile on his lips.

'Sod off,' said Farley.

'I want to see what he's made of. I need protection.'

'You'll be on a charge.' Farley seemed anxious now.

Solly Parker suddenly grabbed Boyd round the waist. 'How about a little wrestle? Just to see what a big strong man you are.'

'Let go,' said Boyd, making no attempt to throw him off. 'If you don't. I'm going to have to restrain you, right along rule book regulations.' But, of course, he didn't know what they were. Why hadn't Brand briefed him properly?

Parker's grip tightened, but Boyd was more conscious of his strong body odour than the strength of his arms.

'Let go,' he repeated.

'Why should I?'

'I've warned you. Can I restrain him?'

'You certainly can,' said Farley.

Boyd put his hand under Parker's chin and began to push upwards. He gave a grunt of pain. But he didn't let go and his grip tightened.

50

'I warned you,' said Boyd, pushing at Parker's chin again, aware that his body odour seemed to be increasing as he exerted himself even more. 'Let me go.' Boyd was all too well aware that if he wasn't careful he could break Solly Parker's neck. Releasing him, he raised his right knee, butted him in the stomach and chopped hard at Parker's neck.

Parker swore and then cried out in pain. His grip slackened and he fell to the floor.

'Now you've gone and done it,' said Jordan admonishingly. 'Let's see you talk your way out of that.'

'What *have* you done?' asked Farley anxiously, staring down at Parker whose legs were flailing in the air.

'Army training,' muttered Boyd. 'He'll come to in a minute and I think I was perfectly justified. The prisoner was attacking me.'

'The prisoner was playing with you,' said Jordan.

'I don't play like that.'

Boyd gazed down at the recumbent figure of Solly Parker, his legs on the floor now and only slightly trembling. Then he opened his eyes.

'Fuck you,' he said.

'I'm sorry. You left me no choice.' He bent down towards Parker as if to help him up, but he rolled over and got to his feet on his own.

'You been in the army?'

'Royal Engineers.'

'Sapper?'

'Sergeant. But I also took some combat training. I'm sorry if I hurt you.'

'I want this logged.' Parker was tense with anger. 'Do you hear me, Farley? I want this logged as assault.'

'It'll be logged as self-defence. That's all.' Farley turned to Boyd. 'That'll be enough for today.'

'Has he met Rhodes?' asked Jordan.

'This morning.'

'He's a right nutter.'

'I thought he was a clever, interesting man,' said Boyd.

51

'Fuck you!' contributed Parker predictably.

'He's lethal,' said Jordan. 'Not Solly – our William. I wonder if he killed Royston and Jones?'

'I think he only goes for rapists,' said Boyd, and Jordan chuckled.

'Maybe he made a mistake with Royston. Let's hope he doesn't make one with us.'

They returned to reception where the shifts were changing over.

'Sorry about that,' said Farley. 'I was a bit slow.'

'Did you want to put me through a test?'

Farley didn't reply, but a prison officer within earshot began to hoot with derisive laughter. 'Of course he did. We had a lot of fun watching you sort out Parker on the monitors. He always tries that on newcomers. I think he finds hugging prison officers a bit of a turn-on.'

'Shut up, Chris,' said Farley, but he was smiling.

'So I *was* on test.'

'Just a little one.'

'Does Parker really do that to everyone?'

'You bet he does,' said Chris amid more laughter.

One of the younger prison officers clapped Boyd on the back as he passed him. 'Did he give you a nice cuddle then?'

'You could say that.'

'He's bent.'

'And stinks,' contributed someone else.

'Is he in some kind of relationship with Jordan?' asked Boyd.

'Yes,' said Bill Farley. 'They've made the best of a bad job, although how Jordan can stand that pungent body odour beats me. Any port in a storm, I suppose.' Farley looked round at the assembled staff. Conversation had stopped and all eyes were on Boyd. 'You'll all have seen Luke acquitting himself well. Parker didn't know what hit him.'

'I'm afraid I wasn't sure what form restraint can take,' said Boyd. 'So I used my discretion.'

There was a roar of laughter as Ted Brand entered the room, looking drained. He glanced at his watch and then at Boyd. 'I'll take you to the governor's office. It's nearly time for your meeting.' His presence seemed to douse the good humour.

Boyd got up, conscious that he had been put to the test and won through, receiving the plaudits of the crowd. He felt almost grateful to Farley now. At least he'd been quickly accepted by his fellow screws and he knew that was a vital step forward.

He got up amidst ragged cheers and scattered applause and followed Ted Brand out of the satellite and through the security procedures to the main prison.

'Don't play to the crowd,' Brand warned him sourly.

'I didn't have much choice,'

'Be your own man.'

'Farley set me up.'

'I sometimes wonder if he's bent,' said Brand. 'Maybe he's too close to some of these inmates.' Brand seemed to be in a particularly bad mood.

'I gather he's divorced.'

'I know – and he's got a daughter at college. Most of us find our hours here overlong. Farley seems to be the exception to that rule.' Brand paused and then continued. 'Anyway, however he feels, he's watched as much as the inmates. He's on CCTV all the time.'

'CCTV that can be turned off,' said Boyd, grabbing the opportunity to stir a little. He was surprised at Brand being so unprofessional.

'Everyone's under constant surveillance,' he repeated.

'That depends on individual commitment of course.' Boyd was stung by Brand's apparent complacency.

'Only been here seconds and already teaching his granny to suck eggs.' But Brand didn't seem put out as he came to a halt outside a door which read GOVERNOR'S OFFICE.

Brand knocked. The corridor was painted a warm orange and hung with pictures of groups of inmates looking, or being, productive. They reminded Boyd of school.

'Come in.'

Brand led Boyd into a beige-carpeted room with modern furniture. Big French windows opened on to smooth green lawns fringed with flowering shrubs.

The man behind the desk came as a slight shock, for he looked more like a stereotypical veteran journalist than a governor, wearing braces, a flamboyant check shirt open at the neck and a pair of sharp chinos.

'This is Taylor, sir. Luke Taylor,' said Brand.

'Come and sit down.' Hathaway was a big man, but by no means running to seed. He had a tanned, unlined face, and well-styled silver-gilt hair. 'Leave him with me, Ted,' he said briskly.

'OK, sir.'

When Brand had gone, Hathaway got up and beckoned Boyd into an adjoining room. He then shut and locked the door, pulled down a blind over a high window and sat down at a small table, indicating that Boyd should take the other chair.

'We're now in a more secure position, Mr Boyd.'

He had wondered how Hathaway was going to play this. On one hand Boyd thought he was taking a risk by seeing him at all, but on the other he was pleased that he was prepared to be so direct.

'How do you appraise the situation?'

Boyd remembered Jordan's summary and realised how right he'd been. 'I think we're offered some options.'

'Which are?'

'The murders were committed by a criminal ring that has some prison officers in its chain of command. Secondly, there could be some kind of management involvement.'

'How would you define that?'

'Someone who's trying to destroy the experiment – and you at the same time.'

'Anything else?'

'Someone on a moral crusade –'

'That sounds like Rhodes.'

'– or some kind of extreme right-wing conspiracy.'

'Where from?'

'Outside, but using prison officers as insiders.'

Hathaway smiled at Boyd, partly encouragingly, partly warily. 'The most likely scenario could be the latter.'

'What makes you think that?'

'A Wing is a radical experiment which could spread into other institutions and some people would love to see my baby choke on its own bile. Then we could return to strict law and order. There's a large number of people who think we're making life easy for cold-blooded killers. The murders could have been committed to prove we're running out of control, that the experiment is security flawed.'

'So how did they get insider help? Brand's sure that the prison officers on the unit are in the clear.'

'He would say that, wouldn't he?'

Boyd nodded. 'So you reckon it *is* an inside job. Someone on the unit killed Jones and Royston and set them up to look as if a moral crusader *is* at work.'

'I've got a gut feeling that the murders were politically motivated, deliberately highlighting the vulnerability of an unpopular innovation.' Hathaway ran a hand through his elegant hairstyle, but it soon sprang back to perfection again. Wasn't he being too glib? wondered Boyd.

'Just how unpopular is the unit?'

'A Wing was politically unpopular well before the plans were even on the drawing board. We were seen to be pandering to some of the most violent criminals in the country. I happen to believe they should be contained – certainly not released – but their environment should make them lead reasonably productive lives.'

Once again, Boyd thought Hathaway sounded slightly fake, or was he just being ingenuous?

'Rhodes seems to be a rather good example of that.'

Hathaway gave him a grim smile. 'Rhodes is the one inmate who shouldn't be here, in my opinion.'

'Why not?'

'I'm sure you've noticed his behaviour is a little unorthodox? Even bizarre?'

'You mean he should be in Broadmoor?'

'I certainly do.'

'What's your own position now?' asked Boyd. 'After the killings.'

'The PM has got the Home Office to put discreet pressure on me to resign.'

'Will you?'

'Not unless I'm more publicly pushed.'

'Could that take time?'

'No. It could happen tomorrow. The press want me to go today, but I've got to hang on in the hope you can make some progress.'

'Time isn't on my side.'

'What about the staff? I know it's early days, but we've got no time at all.'

Boyd related the Parker episode and Hathaway nodded with some approval.

'That was good work.'

'I hope it didn't look like a performance.'

'Be careful.'

'I *am* being careful. But the point is, how long have I really got?'

'A few days. A week at the outside.'

'Christ!'

'I know. But if I have to go, the unit will close – and there's more to it than that. Two lifers have been murdered. The press pack are baying at the gates and the public's lapping it up. The climate will be right for all manner of reactionary "reforms" to be made.'

'There isn't anyone I can trust in the unit –'

'No. And I think you should look carefully at Rhodes.'

'Because he's so single-minded? But he's relocated his obsession. Murder's only for indexing now.'

'I'm concerned about Farley and Rhodes.'

'As a partnership?'

'As manipulator – and manipulated.'

'You reckon *Farley* could have been paid to put Rhodes up to slitting their throats?'

'He has influence over him.'

'Not that I've noticed. Rhodes could certainly be seen as some sort of moral crusader in the past, but now he seems to have switched track to his *magnum opus*. That's all he *appears* to be concerned with now.'

'I disagree.'

'On what grounds?' asked Boyd.

'When Rhodes's sister was murdered, retribution became his central obsession and he rather extended that beyond the call of revenge.'

'And you reckon he could kill again?'

'He wouldn't need much encouragement. Writing is a form of survival for Rhodes. Killing is a pleasure.'

They were silent. Then Boyd said, 'So the murders could have been committed by insiders, possibly, or possibly not, using Rhodes, manipulated by outside political forces. You've set me quite a task – in such a short space of time.' He felt a wave of panic.

'So what's your next move?' asked Hathaway.

'To check out Farley. If your theory's right, we need to see who might be his paymaster.'

'That means moving very fast indeed.'

'Suppose I break into his house tonight?' Boyd was thinking fast, snatching at straws.

'He could well be at home. His shift ends the same time as yours.'

'There's nothing you can do about that? And don't answer – it's a rhetorical question.'

'Report back to me,' said Hathaway. 'I want to stay on here as governor and I need A Wing to survive.'

They shook hands and as he opened the door Neil Hathaway said for the benefit of anyone in the outer office, 'It's good to have you on board, Mr Taylor – and in such difficult circumstances. The very best of luck to you, and, remember, I'm always around if you've got a problem.' He ended on the blandest possible note, but in fact there was only one woman in the office. She was in her mid-thirties with auburn hair and an air of authority. 'This is my personal assistant, Angela Mason.'

'I'm pleased to meet you.'

'And so am I. If you can't get hold of the governor, there's always me.' The slight ambiguity made Boyd give a fleeting smile which was momentarily returned. 'I'm not here to protect Mr Hathaway,' she explained. 'I'm a facilitator.'

Chapter Five

'They make a fine team,' said Farley when Boyd returned to reception on A Wing.

'You mean the governor and his assistant?'

'The governor and his *lovely* assistant.'

He and Farley were alone and Boyd was thankful that the others weren't there to guffaw away in their usual style.

'I liked Hathaway,' said Boyd cautiously. 'He seemed fair and supportive. I also realise his head is on the block.'

'Did he confide?'

'Not at all. But's it's very obvious, isn't it?'

'And how did you rate the fragrant Angie?'

Boyd found it difficult to tell whether Farley was trying to be funny or not. 'She seems to have a lot going for her,' he replied.

'You know she's on the management team?'

'I thought she was his PA.'

'That too.'

Anxious not to waste an opportunity, Boyd smothered a yawn and asked, 'Fancy a drink after work?'

'I'd love to, but I've got a date tonight. I'm meeting someone in a restaurant and may be late home.'

'Another time then?' said Boyd, wondering why Farley was so expansive with the information on his private life.

'I'll look forward to it,' said Farley.

None of the three remaining lifers appeared in the association area that evening. Farley had given Boyd a large amount of paperwork to familiarise himself with, which needed filling in on his next shift, so he sat for a long time at a desk in reception, checking that he understood the procedures and watching each of the three prisoners in their pods on CCTV.

William Rhodes was working at his desk, turning over documents, consulting reference books, making notes and referring back. To all intents and purposes he was totally engrossed.

So was Solly Parker, who was lying on his bed reading a magazine called *Adonis*, eagerly turning over the pages. Jon Jordan was watching a comedy show on TV, although he showed no signs of amusement.

Boyd didn't take long to find Bill Farley's address in the files, which was listed as 14 Taunton Terrace. Checking the A-Z he discovered the terrace was only a few streets away. How convenient, he thought, planning to break into the house later that evening, although he knew the chances of finding something incriminating were thin.

Then he saw Bill Farley on Rhodes's CCTV monitor. He had reached the desk and was standing there, waiting for Rhodes to look up. He made no attempt to bring himself to his attention and gave the impression of being a rather over-deferential butler.

Scrabbling through his piles of paper, Rhodes eventually produced what looked like a list which he gave to Farley. He glanced at it for a moment, nodded and then walked slowly towards the steel shutter.

Boyd hurried over to the desk, anticipating Farley's return, going through his paperwork yet again, shoving the scrap of paper on which he had written Farley's address into his pocket.

When he returned a few minutes later, Boyd was still bent over the documentation.

'Savvy?' Farley seemed distracted.

'Yes. It's all pretty clear.'

'I'll do them tonight. Then you can do the next set tomorrow.'

'I'll fill them in if you like,' said Boyd. 'I know you're out for a night on the tiles.'

There was a slight pause. 'I wouldn't say that. Let's stick to what I said.' He sounded slightly uneasy and Boyd backed off.

'OK.'

Farley picked up the papers and walked over to another desk. He sat down and began to methodically fill in the documents.

Boyd returned to the monitors, but nothing had changed. Rhodes was as busy as ever, Jordan continued to watch the comedy show, still without showing the slightest pleasure, and Parker thumbed through his handsome hunk magazine with what appeared to be increasing interest.

Several prison officers came into the room and Farley went to join them as they gathered round one of the other monitors.

'Time for wanking.'

'Just watch him jerk off.'

'What's going on?' asked Boyd.

'Watch that space,' said Farley.

Suddenly, Solly Parker turned over on his back, pulled his tracksuit trousers down and began to masturbate, seemingly oblivious to the cameras.

'Doesn't he know we're watching?' asked Boyd.

'He knows,' laughed Farley. 'But he doesn't give a sod. I mean – would you? These CCTV cameras are on all the time.'

Boyd suddenly felt revolted, but far more by the voyeuristic attitude of the staff than Parker's enjoyment. Maybe I'd do the same thing, thought Boyd, if I knew I was on camera all day. But he knew he couldn't afford to be fastidious, not if he wanted to be 'one of the boys'.

A great cheer went up as Solly Parker arched his back and, with a salacious grin at the camera, ejaculated as hard as he could.

Then he raised two fingers in the air, pulled off his tracksuit trousers and went into his bathroom.

'There's still the blind spot then,' said Boyd to Farley. 'Why doesn't Hathaway do something about that?'

'Because he's sticking to his original philosophy. We've got men on every shutter. There's no way anyone could get at him.'

'Who got at the others?' asked Boyd. 'And how?'

'We didn't have staff posted on every shutter.'

'But how did the killer get in? He would have been seen on the cameras.'

'All right, Poirot,' said Farley. 'Don't strain those little grey cells too much.'

Boyd realised his cross-examination had been far too premature. He'd have to be more careful or he'd start to arouse suspicion. The problem remained, however, that he was having to move much faster than he should.

As Boyd stole through the dark streets to Bill Farley's house he still felt revolted by the laughing and cheering prison officers who had been watching Parker masturbating. Their attitude had made Boyd feel soiled and he couldn't keep Solly Parker's long, thin body out of his mind as he threshed about on the bed, defying his audience. Yet there had even been a strange dignity to his masturbation and Boyd felt a sense of self-loathing.

He eventually found the South London terrace he'd been looking for, gentrified, prettified, some of the houses with a pink or grey or even a jasmine-coloured wash. Number 14 was one of the most attractive – matt yellow, with window boxes full of geraniums. The steps had been painted white and there was a gleaming brass door knocker that shone in the moonlight.

Boyd kept walking, turning right into another, more run-down street, doubling back on himself to check the back garden of 14 Taunton Terrace which was enclosed by a fence painted light green. There was even a garden gate.

Looking round and making sure he was unobserved. Boyd leapt over the gate and made his way down the fastidiously swept path to the back door. He picked the lock, and taking care not to make the slightest sound he opened the door. Boyd then flashed his pencil beam torch around the interior of the neat kitchen, surfaces clean and clear, the fridge humming and the red light of the central heating a small beacon.

Ensuring his torch beam was kept as low as possible, Boyd began to search each room, opening bureaux and cabinets and checking through the drawers of a desk. The place was elegantly furnished, with reproduction furniture – or at least Boyd imagined it was, for how could Farley buy genuine antiques with the salary of a prison officer? But the more he looked around the ground floor of the house, the more he began to wonder if he was actually looking at the genuine article.

So far his search had revealed nothing and there was a personal sterility to it all, without a trace of history of any kind.

Then Boyd began to climb the stairs. The walls were covered in small prints showing wild flowers, beautifully executed, and he wondered if the watercolours had been painted by Farley himself.

Boyd reached into his jacket pocket and pulled out the balaclava mask that he'd also brought with him, and should have put on when he had first broken into the house. What the hell was the matter with him? Why was he being so slipshod and careless? At least he had remembered to put on the gloves.

There were three rooms upstairs, one of which was painted a warm orange, and the second a leaf green, but

63

although he checked thoroughly he still couldn't find anything personal. Boyd returned to the landing and froze. Hadn't he just heard a faint sound like a light snore?

Had Farley returned? Had he never gone out in the first place? And what was Boyd going to do? There was still one bedroom left to search. A wild curiosity seized him, surprisingly followed by a rush of sexual desire for Marcia. Again he saw the disturbing image of Parker's long lean body masturbating on the bed, almost like a theatrical performance with its contemptible audience – a contemptible audience that had included himself.

Boyd paused and then saw the door opposite was open a crack. He pushed gently and saw a double bed. Switching off his torch, he peered inside and noticed a hunched figure. Was this Farley? Or a lover? A lover who if Brand was to be believed could well be male. Boyd crept further into the room. The curtains hadn't been drawn and the moon was full, shining through the window on to the bed, lighting up the face of a young woman.

At first he thought she was a child. Boyd felt a sense of shock and then wondered if she could be Farley's daughter. She was incredibly small.

Slowly, cautiously, Boyd withdrew from the neat bedroom with its pine cupboards and pot pourri in jars on the dressing table. He edged his way along the landing, down the stairs and paused by the living-room door. Should he search again? But he knew he'd be taking too much of a risk.

Boyd crept into the kitchen and made for the door, which he opened noiselessly. Then he readjusted the lock and, checking to make sure he was safe, hurried down the garden path. He passed a sundial, and in the moonlight saw the serrated message carved into its surface. When he flashed the pencil beam he read: IT's LATER THAN YOU THINK.

The message held a grim truth.

* * *

64

When Boyd got back to the flat he felt another rush of physical desire for Marcia. He poured himself a tumbler of iced orange juice, drained the contents and went outside again, hurrying down the road to a phone box.

She answered at once. Had she been hoping he'd ring?

'Marcia?'

'Thank God you phoned.'

'I've only been away a day.'

'I know.'

'You missing me?'

'Like crazy.'

Boyd felt a rush of adrenalin.

'How long's this job going to last?'

'I don't know. Not long.'

'Look, Danny, I've got to ask you . . .'

'About what?'

'Is there any chance of us living together?'

'Yes. God, yes!' He felt a sudden, overwhelming joy.

'You mean it?'

'I most certainly do. It's so strange . . .'

'What is?'

'That we not only survived the dry-out, but met again and found we really needed each other.' Boyd paused. 'I really mean what I say,' he added, trying to reassure her.

'I know. I can tell by the tone of your voice.'

'I'm very sure.'

'So am I. It's like a miracle. What will you do if we – when we live together?'

'Do you mean will I still take on this kind of work? No, of course I won't. I was only an insider to try and – to try and forget what happened.' Boyd spoke slowly and unsteadily. He had not felt happiness like this for what seemed an eternity. How fragile the emotion seemed, he thought. Like gauze or puff-balls drifting in a breeze. 'But it never worked. And this time, I can't slip into another identity as easily as I did, and I've made some mistakes. That's all your fault.'

'You've got to be careful.'

'I will – now I know I've got a future. You *really* are sure, aren't you?'

'Yes. Completely sure. We must trust each other. Can't you get out of this job?'

'No. I'd never get a transfer back to the Met if I did. It's crucial.'

'But you're in danger.'

'Yes.' He wanted to be honest with her. 'But it's not going to last long. There's one hell of a deadline.'

'I can't bear it.'

'You'll have to. So will I. But once this case's over, that's it.'

'Will you hanker after the – the –'

'Excitement's the wrong word. I've never found being an insider exciting, and as I said, trying to blot out the past was never successful. They're dead. I have to accept that – and the blame. The pain will never go away, but now I've got the chance of a new life I won't let you go.'

'When can I see you?'

'When it's over.'

'But you'll keep in touch?'

'I'll phone you when I can. I love you.'

'You've never said that before.'

'I *love* you.'

'I love you, Danny. I love you so much. When can you contact me again?'

'Tomorrow.'

'Remember the strength of my love. Maybe it'll keep you safe.'

They both hung up and Boyd went out into the darkness of the street and looked up at the moon.

He had touched happiness. The experience was exhilarating.

Chapter Six

HM Prison Aston
22 June 2001 – 0730 hours

When Boyd arrived at the prison next day, security had been tightened up still further and he had to have identity clearance at least three times.

Eventually he entered the unit feeling tired and apprehensive, every instinct telling him that something was about to go badly wrong. The premonition was fulfilled immediately.

As he walked into reception he was buttonholed by Ted Brand. 'Farley's reported sick. He's inclined to bad migraines, but he's hardly ever away for more than a day at a time. What I'd like you to do is to take over his duties. I realise that's plunging you in at the deep end.'

'What *are* his duties?'

'Rhodes.'

'How long does he spend with him?'

'The mornings, usually. I expect you realise he's got quite a special relationship with him. He also manages to keep Rhodes calm.'

'Calm?' Boyd was decidedly nervous. 'What does Rhodes do when he *isn't* calm? Indulge in a little cannibalism?'

'That's Hannibal Lector.' Brand was impatient. 'Leave that to the realms of fiction. Rhodes has bouts of rage, but I've never known him to be physically violent.'

'He only cuts up his victims, but don't let's call that violence. How about surgery?'

'I'm talking about his behaviour patterns on A Wing.'

'He won't be very pleased to find his research assistant is away.'

'He'll have to put up with that for a day. But I thought this would be a good opportunity for you to get started with him.'

'OK,' said Boyd with a confidence he didn't feel. 'How's the CID investigation proceeding?'

'Slowly. There was full staffing when Royston and Jones were murdered, although I wasn't on shift myself. Both men were found dead on the toilet; Royston in the early hours of the morning and Jones the following afternoon. You'll have heard about the "break from viewing" everyone apparently takes when my back's turned. That could have accounted for Royston. But what I don't understand is how the CCTV was turned off – even for a few moments – when Jones was killed. During the night all the monitors are watched by a duty officer.'

'Who was on?'

'Farley. He apparently went to take a leak twice, but he wouldn't have been away for long. Anyway, he told the police that one of the other officers took over each time he left – Warwick on the first occasion, and Slade on the second. They've both been questioned, but there's been no result.'

Boyd was aware that Brand wanted to unburden himself to a new face and a fresh pair of ears.

'Can the cameras be switched off from reception?'

'Of course. The control centre is here. But the inmates are on camera all the time, except for the toilet area. So if anyone was anywhere else in the pods they'd have been seen on the monitors at once.'

'Apart from going to the toilet there's not a moment when the inmates *aren't* on camera?'

'Only if the computer or power supply goes down.

But we've got back-up cameras and monitors to each pod and we record on DVD with automatic back-up and change-over.'

Boyd wondered if he should try to stop the conversation, but he still had the impression that Brand needed to talk the subject through, that he had been racking his brains alone for too long and had become obsessed with the problem. Boyd knew he needed to take advantage of this without overplaying his hand. It was very subtle – and very alarming. He could give himself away too easily.

'And you're really sure that no member of staff could have been in collusion with an inmate? You said you had a gut feeling about Rhodes . . .'

'I've known these guys for a long time. They've had massive security clearances and there are checks all the time. You're the first new member of staff we've had on A Wing for some time.' Then Brand changed tack. 'You ought to consider yourself lucky. You've had no experience working in any kind of prison, yet here you are on the top security unit.' Brand stared at him rather curiously. 'Your army training's counted – witness the restraint you managed to put on Solly Parker.'

'Where do your new officers usually come from?'

'They get experience in other departments of the prison system until they're ready to apply and be considered for A Wing. Of course, in the present circumstances recruitment would be difficult.'

Boyd decided to change the subject, which was getting too reflective. 'The recording equipment must have developed a fault.'

'Either that or one of the cameras did.'

'There's no record –'

'The log doesn't show a damn thing,' Brand went over to the coffee percolator and poured out a couple of cups. 'Just have a coffee and listen to me for a while, Luke. I've got this feeling that if Rhodes is mad, then I'm mad too. All I do is think about what might have happened. I can't get the permutations out of my mind – not that there *are* that many. OK, there were no cameras in the toilet, a hitch with the computer and some unauthorised non-viewing, but how the fuck were they got at?' Brand paused and then said, 'I've already bent the wife's ear until she can hardly take any more. Suppose – just suppose – there *is* an insider. Even several insiders?'

You've certainly scored there, thought Boyd. Bingo. Got it in one. 'It's a possibility,' he said. 'But I thought you said they all have maximum security clearance.'

'They do.' Brand was clearly weakening. 'But how safe *is* maximum security clearance? I'm beginning to wonder . . .'

Boyd felt that he had made a breakthrough at last. Brand had been so sure his staff were invincible that he had deliberately blinded himself to the idea that Boyd had begun to favour himself. Now they were getting somewhere. If the result was important enough, then the insiders would have been well set up and highly paid – unlike himself. How much was the closure of the unit worth? How much was Neil Hathaway's dismissal worth? To a group totally focused on the law and order issue, to a group insistent that violent criminals should be punished and not treated as human beings, the price could be a very high one.

'Conspiracy,' said Brand with a painful smile. 'That's what we could be dealing with. As I said, A Wing is political dynamite, but it would seem the CID are light years away from a solution.' Brand drained his coffee. 'You must think I'm a real old woman, maundering on like this, but as every day passes I'm becoming increasingly apprehensive. We're all going to lose our jobs. You could be the shortest-term prison officer we've ever had. Sorry about that, Luke.'

'Who else believes in the conspiracy theory?' asked Boyd.

'It's unacceptable to the staff.'

'And publicly you're denying the possibility?'

'You bet I am.'

'While actually believing in the idea?'

70

'What else is left?' Brand was impatient. 'We've eliminated all other theories.'

'The question is, how did they go about it? Maybe your hunch about Rhodes was right and he was used.'

Brand shrugged. 'You know what he's like. He only has one obsession.'

'He had another one once. He wanted to kill. Maybe the history book is a front and he still has his old agenda.'

'That would need staff collusion on a huge scale.' Brand was becoming increasingly irritated, and Boyd guessed that he was regretting a confidence to such a new and junior prison officer.

'Shall I go and make Bill Farley's apologies to Rhodes?'

'Do just that. And I apologise for going on.'

'Don't. It's good to talk to you and hear your thoughts –'

'Which are completely circular.'

'There *will* be an explanation,' said Boyd. 'I'm sure the police will come up with something soon.'

'They'd better,' said Brand.

'Any useful tips you can give me on Rhodes?'

'Go in and listen to him. He may have been a violent man once, but he's just like a big pussy-cat here.'

'I don't think I'll start stroking him,' said Boyd.

'That could be a mistake,' said Brand drily. 'If you get stuck for conversation, you could ask him if he needs any more typing paper. I usually give him some of the office stock.'

'That's generous – as long as you don't give him any with the prison heading.'

Brand had the grace to smile faintly. 'He wouldn't mind as long as he can write on it. Rhodes isn't choosy.'

Boyd felt incredibly exposed as he operated his laser key

71

on the walkway, accompanied by salacious encouragement from his colleagues.

'Go and kiss his arse then.'

'Don't call him by his first name – not until he gives you permission. He doesn't like familiarity.'

'He's a bit touchy about his past.'

'Don't mention his sister.'

Boyd became apprehensive as he approached the pod. He felt very alone and Rhodes's absorption was chilling. If he had been as single-minded in his quest for retribution as he was in his research, then Rhodes was a force to be reckoned with.

Reaching the steel shutter, he spoke into the entryphone. When he received no response he aimed his laser and the shutter slid up, smoothly and silently.

Rhodes's head was bent over his papers and he didn't look up.

'I'm sorry,' said Boyd. 'Bill Farley's got a migraine.'

Rhodes turned and gazed up at him, looking put out.

'He's not coming in?'

'Not today.'

'Shit! Shit and double shit. The man's an arsehole.'

'He hardly asked to have a migraine,' said Boyd drily.

Rhodes went back to his work.

'He'll be in tomorrow.'

Rhodes frowned and turned over the page in a large and densely written manuscript.

'Can I do anything for you?' asked Boyd cautiously, pushing a little harder.

Rhodes cleared his throat and then looked up again. For a minute Boyd was surprised by his blank expression and the distant look in his eyes. Everyday tasks were of no interest to him, he seemed to be saying. Nothing must be allowed to sway him from the work in hand.

'Does Mr Farley change your books in the prison library here?' Boyd persisted.

'What?'

Boyd repeated the question slowly, suddenly wondering if Rhodes was trying to wind him up. 'Does he change them in the library here?'

'For God's sake!'

'What have I said?'

'Are you shit stupid?'

'I hope not.' Although he was determined not to let Rhodes walk all over him. Boyd felt increasingly afraid of the driven power of the man.

'Someone walk over your grave?'

Boyd said nothing.

'Are you afraid of me?'

'Of course not.'

'I despise people who are afraid of me.'

'All I want to know is –'

'Listen, my friend. Bill isn't frightened of me. In fact we're buddies. Both Williams, Sweet Williams.' Rhodes gave a self-satisfied chuckle. 'The problem is,' he said slowly, as if talking to a particularly stupid child, 'the prison library is only for shitheads.'

'Really?'

'Are you challenging my judgement?'

'Perhaps.' Boyd was determined to stand up to him.

'Have you *been* in the library?'

'No.'

'It's full of fiction. Full of lies. Fiction is a lie.'

'A lot of people like reading fiction.'

'Then they're shitheads.'

'Of course you need history. Non-fiction.'

'What is your history?'

'I don't understand –'

'Exactly.' Rhodes leant back in his chair and ran a hand through his unruly hair.

'So you're saying the prison library isn't sufficiently well stocked for your needs.'

'As you know, I have a subscription to the London Library. Bill is my winged messenger for ancillary reading.'

73

'Can I fill the gap?'

'What do you mean?'

'I've no doubt Mr Brand will allow me to go to the library for you. Providing he can spare me on the shift, of course.'

'So you'll run an errand?'

'I could do.'

'Then I need you to go this morning. I need Brunswick's *Feudal England*. I think I've missed a reference.' Rhodes sounded impatient with himself. 'I only had the book last week.'

'It's easy to make a –'

'A mistake is very irritating, especially to a man in my position.' His speech was rather arcane – as if he had some trouble in communicating. Suppose his writing was gibberish?

Boyd moved cautiously to a position where he could see the manuscript.

'What are you doing?' Rhodes was irritable.

'Sorry?'

'You're moving about.'

'I didn't mean –'

'Spying on my work.'

'I'm just interested.'

'Are you checking on me?'

'Of course not. Why should I?'

'Instructions from on high?'

Boyd froze.

'When one gets a higher instruction one has to obey.'

'Meaning?' What was Rhodes trying to say? Or was he simply rambling? Surely he should have been sent to Broadmoor.

'A higher instruction, on a national or even spiritual level – we must all obey that,' said Rhodes quietly. 'Obviously. Do you think I'm a madman? That I wouldn't be able to obey when the call comes?'

'What can I get you from the library?'

'I just told you – Brunswick's *Feudal England*.' He was

74

angry, clearly reckoning that Boyd was both slow and stupid.

'Is there anything else?'

'If you'd just get that you'd be of more use than standing there, spying on my work, regardless of my sensibilities.'

'I'm sorry,' said Boyd. He was genuinely contrite. 'I didn't mean to spy. I'm just terribly interested in what you're writing. History fascinates me, and of course Bill – Mr Farley – has great respect for you. He told me something of your work. Only a little.' Boyd paused, hoping Rhodes might open up.

'Mr Farley is a good man.'

'Yes, I . . .'

There was a long pause. 'Well?'

'Er . . .' Boyd had dried up and panic was setting in. What was he going to say? He had to say *something*. But no words would come and the panic was replaced by a terror that Boyd had not felt in a long while. A terror of the unknown, a nameless dread that he couldn't fathom.

'Is there something the matter?' asked Rhodes.

'You scared me.' Boyd couldn't even think of a lie.

'Yes.'

'What do you mean – yes?'

'I mean I understand. I know people find me formidable. Perhaps it's because I'm a natural solitary, so my environment doesn't depress me in the least. But I'm here – at Her Majesty's expense. I inhabit my pod. I bury myself in my work. And that pleases me.'

'Your work *is* very interesting.'

'You're not trying to curry favour?'

'No,' said Boyd, regaining some composure. 'I'm certainly afraid – maybe for the reasons you've just described – but I see no reason to curry favour.'

'Even if I said I'd chop you up into little bits?' Rhodes chuckled.

There was another pause.

'I mean – that's what I used to do before I became an

75

historian. But I don't chop history into little bits. I write down what happened. Churchill's version was abridged. By his own hand, of course. I don't mean an editorial hand.'

'No,' said Boyd dutifully, trying to find an opening to get the conversation back to the question of a 'higher authority'.

'What are you doing now?' asked Rhodes irritably.

'What do you mean?'

'What are you doing? You're standing there with no purpose. Go and get me my library book.'

'Before I go, there's just one thing . . .'

'What is that one thing?'

'The business of a higher authority. That you would obey.'

'Yes?'

'What did you mean, higher authority?'

'Mr Farley and I – have to subscribe to authority from time to time. If a deed has to be done, and done quickly, I'm ready to do my duty.'

'Is this duty – is this to do with your sister?'

For a moment their eyes met and Boyd had the distinct impression that Rhodes was ready to explode.

But he was wrong.

Instead, Rhodes smiled. 'She was my beloved. And on behalf of my beloved I had to take action.' There was a trace of anxiety in his voice and hesitation in his expression.

'Have I got this right? A higher authority asked you to commit violent acts, and you think you may be asked to do them again?'

'I won't talk in this way.'

'You can with me.'

'What purpose would that serve?'

'That you'll still be safe to carry out your researches in the privacy of your own environment. That you'll be undisturbed.'

'I was guaranteed privacy.'

'Was that after you'd obeyed the instructions?'

'I gave you instructions to get me a library book. I might as well howl to the moon. I shall have to take this further.'

'To a higher authority?' Boyd knew he was pushing him to the limit.

'I need my peace. I need my library book. And can you get me half a pound of cube sugar?' Rhodes suddenly seemed much more vulnerable.

'I can get that for you right away.'

'Chewing a lump of sugar is good for the concentration. It melts in the mouth.'

'Will canteen sugar lumps do?'

'They'll have to. Any port in a storm.'

'Are you in a storm?'

'What are you talking about now? You do talk an awful lot of rubbish for such a clever young man.'

'Do you have a library ticket?'

'Of course.' Rhodes got to his feet and pulled out an empty drawer. He shook it impatiently and a library ticket slid forward from the back. 'Guard this well. I'd hate to have the embarrassment of losing a ticket. That would cause a good many complications.'

Boyd took the ticket and smiled at Rhodes. To his surprise, Rhodes smiled back.

'I hope I can work with you,' Boyd said slowly.

'As Mr Farley's assistant? Or apprentice, perhaps? I'm sure there's room for a young man of intelligence. I'll talk to Mr Farley when he's recovered. And now – off to the library with you. I need that book before I take a siesta.'

'I'll go now.'

Boyd pointed his laser key at the shutter which slid up with merciful speed.

'How was he?' asked Brand, who seemed more composed when Boyd returned from his encounter with Rhodes.

'He told me to get him a library book.'

'Then you'd better go right away. He's never asked any other of the staff to do that. I'm sure he doesn't have the prison library in mind.'

'He doesn't think too highly of the prison library.'

'No – he wouldn't, and he's right. I'm glad you got along with him. Bill's been the only one so far.'

As Boyd made his way towards the next steel shutter he had only one thought. Who had placed Rhodes in the unit? Had there been a plan and a purpose? Who was this higher authority?

For the first time in his investigation Boyd thought he was in with a chance.

After Boyd had successfully collected Rhodes's library book, he went into a call box and managed to get through to Creighton.

'How's it going?'

'I've just been borrowing a library book for William Rhodes.'

'Glad you're spending your time usefully. What have you found out?'

'I'm beginning to wonder if Royston and Jones were killed for political reasons.'

'That's rather radical.'

'I know. But everything seems to be pointing to the killings heading up a campaign to close A Wing.'

'There are plenty of other ways pressure could have been brought to bear.'

'I know that too. But I can only go on what I've discovered so far. What's more, William Rhodes should never have been sent to Aston. He's very disturbed.'

'Maybe he got that way.'

'I doubt it.'

'Do you think Rhodes murdered Royston and Jones?'

'He'd have needed help.'

'How do you assess Rhodes – apart from suggesting he should be transferred to Broadmoor?'

'Rhodes has been talking about having to obey a higher authority. He seems to be a single-minded obsessive and would have been diagnosed as a paranoid schizophrenic if the normal procedures had been in place.'

'And you're saying they weren't?'

'They can't have been.'

'But this is a hugely serious charge. You mean that someone deliberately placed Rhodes in the maximum security unit at Aston to carry out a series of murders to close that same unit?'

'That's a possible scenario – except I can't back it up with any evidence.'

'Who would go to such lengths?'

'A law and order fanatic, or a right wing group who wanted to disgrace Hathaway and have the unit closed.'

'They'd have to be influential. What kind of stone would they crawl out from? The government? The prison service?'

'Whoever it is, they could be aiming to keep their own hands clean and manipulate the system in a way I don't yet understand. There are CCTV cameras everywhere and they're never turned off. Theoretically. But there's a blind spot. There isn't a camera in the toilet – and both men were found dead on the toilet.'

'So what are you going to do?'

'I'm going to keep talking to Rhodes. He's developing a history project and I'm the sorcerer's apprentice. There's another prison officer called Bill Farley who's become a research assistant to Rhodes. I think he might be involved in the conspiracy.'

'How?'

'I don't know yet, but I broke into his house last night.'

'Find anything?'

'Only a girl asleep in his bed. I think she was his

daughter in which case she must be in her early twenties. But she was very small. More like a child.'

'What's that meant to indicate?'

'I don't know.'

'Did you disturb her?'

'No.'

Creighton paused. 'You should know that Neil Hathaway is about to resign.'

Boyd let the bombshell burst into a pool of silence.

'That's bad. I was brought in far too late.'

'The news is under wraps at the moment, but might hit the late editions of the evening papers and the news.'

'What is the official line?'

'Ill health. But the point is, why should it be so important to close the unit?'

'A Wing's being seen as a soft option,' said Boyd. 'And there's a lot of demand for a more punitive regime. The crime rate's rising, but banging up dangerous criminals on a wing that treats them with respect – that might seem to pander to their every whim – isn't exactly what the public wants to hear.'

'The Home Secretary's all for A Wing.' Creighton paused. 'But maybe you're right. The conspiracy theory's growing on me.'

'Can Hathaway's resignation be put on hold – in the light of what we think might be happening?'

'I don't know. I'll see what can be done. Meanwhile, I can't help thinking that prison officers becoming research assistants to a serial killer isn't exactly what the public would like to hear either, so don't mention your role to anyone.'

'Rhodes of course is all for law and order,' said Boyd. 'An eye for an eye . . .'

'Quite. But how could he get out of his cell, murder two fellow lifers and wander back in again? It's a very unlikely scenario, isn't it? As you say, CCTV coverage is in place all the time, except for the toilet. I am right in thinking that, am I?'

'Security can't have been that good,' said Boyd.

'But the wing's so heavily staffed. What are you suggesting?'

'Long-term planning. For Jones's murder they could have been counting on the fact that when a prisoner's under escort the other screws take a break from viewing. And instead of tapping in a security code to open the shutters they seem to use a laser key that overrides all security systems. There was also a convenient computer breakdown.'

'Equipment failure would have been logged. Wasn't it?'

'No.'

'Interesting. What do you make of that?'

'I'm working on it.'

'You'd better work faster. Maybe I can get this resignation put on hold – but not for long.'

'I'll report back.'

'Do that. And get to know as much as you can about Rhodes – even if it does mean changing his library books.'

A few minutes later, Boyd called Marcia, praying she would be at home. She was, of course. 'Don't you ever go out?'

'Not if I think there's a chance you're going to ring.'

'You can't just sit there.'

'Try me. How much longer are you going to be?'

'I still don't know.'

'I'm sorry, I shouldn't be badgering you. What have you been doing?'

'Changing a library book for a lunatic.'

'Do I take that literally?'

'It's the lunatic's library book.'

'Don't talk in riddles,' said Marcia sharply.

81

'I'm sorry.'

'You'll keep yourself safe for me –'

'You know I will. I'll ring directly I know when the operation's going to be over.'

'I love you, Danny.'

Chapter Seven

'Thank you,' said Rhodes as Boyd gave him *Feudal England*. 'It's always a pleasure to see an old friend return.' He glanced at the piles of books on his desk and Boyd felt his delight. In fact, Rhodes's pleasure gave *him* pleasure, and for a moment he looked almost affectionately down at the scholar. Then he remembered how Rhodes had also cut up the bodies of those he had killed and scattered the parts in cleansing rivers. There could be no doubt that Rhodes was thorough.

Boyd reminded himself that he mustn't lose the opportunity of these moments. He had to try to get closer to Rhodes, to assess what he might still be capable of doing.

'Are you pleased?' asked Boyd tentatively.

'Very.'

'You don't miss your freedom –'

'It wasn't freedom,' said Rhodes. 'I had to reorder the world on behalf of my sister.'

'Reorder?'

'The world is a filthy place,' said Rhodes. 'There have been predators on the face of the planet since the dawn of time. Predators who seek to destroy all that is innocent.'

Rhodes glanced up at Boyd who thought – or imagined – he saw the obsession in his eyes. But was it for

83

killing, or the great task of history? Or both? Could they be interchangeable?

'I shall be more than content to read and write for the rest of my life. I wouldn't want to be outside Aston.'

'You like it in here?'

'I need to be kept safe. I don't want to leave my pod. Not for a moment.'

'How do you manage that?'

Rhodes didn't give him a direct answer. 'I don't want to go into the association room. I don't want to associate.'

'I don't suppose it's much fun –'

'Not with Jordan and Parker around. They disgust me.'

'Why's that?'

'They've settled for nothing, and even that's mocked by those pathetic shits who pass themselves off as prison officers.'

Boyd couldn't have agreed more. Then he decided that as he seemed to have been approved he'd take the risk of being honest. 'I agree.'

'You do?' Rhodes looked genuinely surprised.

'I heard them – saw them – laughing.'

'Bastards. Jordan and Parker have never been able to keep their dignity and that's why I don't associate with them.'

Rhodes was talking more rationally now and there was no reference to being instructed by a higher authority. That had seemed the peak of his paranoia and Boyd suddenly wondered if he had made a wrong judgement and a bad blunder. Was the higher authority simply part of Rhodes's madness? Rhodes was definitely crazy. He shouldn't be at Aston. He should be in Broadmoor.

'So what about Royston and Jones? Were they any better company?'

'They were animals, but they left me alone. I need to complete my work. I have to live long enough to do that.'

'You don't feel you're in danger?'

'What *is* all this?' asked Rhodes, suddenly sounding disconcertingly human.

'I'm just trying to get to know you.'

'On what basis?'

'On the basis of someone who cares for another person's privacy – and individuality.'

'You sound like Farley.'

'He's a good man.'

'One of the best,' said Rhodes with conviction. 'That's why I stay.' He laughed at his own joke. 'And I don't mind you either. I won't call you by your Christian name yet. I never do that until I can assess the possibility of a person giving me bullshit.'

'The conditions you had to live under in the past must have been much worse.'

'I can assure you they were. I like Hathaway, but I suspect he's not going to be around for long.'

Boyd knew that he had to keep the conversation going, had to convince Rhodes that he was on his side. But he was still considerably surprised by Rhodes's sudden and unexpected grip on reality.

'You're certain he'll be forced to resign?'

'You've probably seen the press. You've noted the law and order backlash. This is the only lifer unit that's been humanely designed. For what I did, had to do, I expected punishment. But I've had plenty of that in the past.'

'What kind of punishment?'

'Countless attacks by prisoners and screws.' He suddenly began to unbutton his shirt and roll up his sleeves to reveal considerable scar tissue on his chest and burns on his arms. Had that happened in secure units, Boyd wondered, or had Rhodes mutilated himself? 'Here on A Wing I've been treated humanely and I'm ready to serve my life sentence and take my punishment.'

'But *are* you being punished?' risked Boyd. 'You are free to read and write. You're fed and watered. You don't have to pay for any services.'

'True.'

'So what sort of punishment would you get in one of the run-of-the-mill units?'

'I wouldn't be allowed to read or write, and I'd be forced to go into the association areas and mix with filth. Isn't that bad enough?'

'Do you ever take advantage of the outside exercise area?'

'Yes. I do ask to be taken there.'

'Does that give you a different environment to think in?'

'I don't think there. There's too much wire. But I look up at the sky and I like to watch the clouds sailing by.' Rhodes paused. 'The political unpopularity of Neil Hathaway is entirely based on a reaction to his humanity. The public don't like humanity. And, with an eye to the election, neither does the government.'

'You think he'll be forced to resign?'

'If he hasn't already. Now, I'm sorry – I have to finish our conversation and get to work again. But thank you for giving me a rather better association period than is currently available. I'd like to talk again, but not now. I don't want to fall behind.'

Boyd got up. 'I've enjoyed this morning. I'll go about my duties.'

'And if Mr Farley's still indisposed tomorrow, please join me for a little while. You may have to run another errand.'

'To the library?'

'And perhaps the post office.'

'I'd be delighted.' Boyd pointed his laser key at the steel shutter. As he went out he muttered, 'Goodbye.'

'Goodbye,' said Rhodes. 'Keep well.'

Closing the shutter, Boyd saw that Rhodes's head was already bent over his desk.

What *is* punishment? wondered Boyd. As far as the law and order lobby was concerned, Rhodes hadn't been punished enough. He was happy in his work.

*   *   *

When Boyd got back to reception he saw that he had been so engrossed with Rhodes that he had almost missed his lunch break. Hurrying over to the canteen he found a seat at a table already occupied by Ted Brand and one of the other younger officers, Ben Maxwell. Clutching a plate of steak and kidney pie, he returned and sat down.

'How's the investigation going?' asked Boyd tentatively.

'It seems to have ground to a halt.' Ted Brand was full of doom.

'So you're chums with Rhodes then?' asked Ben Maxwell. He looked rather put out.

'I seem to have been taken on as an apprentice.'

'Must be difficult for you, coming into a high security unit like this,' said Ben. 'Without any experience of other prisons. Even this one.'

'I suppose they thought they'd drop me in the deep end.'

'Ex-army background,' said Brand. 'That's what counted. So you're actually getting on with Rhodes, are you? He usually gives me a torrent of abuse.'

If Brand knew about Hathaway's resignation he gave nothing away.

'Maybe he doesn't like figures of authority,' observed Ben.

'I don't imagine he thinks I'm a figure of authority,' said Boyd. 'More like an errand boy.'

'He doesn't take to everyone.' Ted Brand sounded slightly anxious. 'So you and Bill should think yourselves lucky.'

'How come he's able to have such an extensive collection of books and papers?' asked Boyd curiously, trying to play devil's advocate. 'Aren't we pandering to him?'

'He's misplaced,' said Ben. 'Should be in the nuthouse.'

'I don't think we're pandering,' said Brand. 'It's important the inmates are kept busy.'

'He's happy.'

'In his own world?' Brand laughed. 'Yes, I guess he is. But he won't last long here. In fact I've applied for his transfer to Broadmoor. Rhodes has become increasingly unstable lately.'

'You didn't mention that before.'

'It's been under wraps. The shrink's seen him a couple of times. He reckons he's schizo and we can't cope with that kind of inmate here.' There seemed to be a note of triumph in Brand's voice.

'And we don't want to,' said Ben. 'To be honest, Rhodes has always scared me shitless, and I'm really beginning to wonder if someone *did* let him loose on Royston and Jones. God knows how though.'

'No one could have let him loose,' said Brand irritably. 'You know damned well he was in his pod when those killings took place. Don't stir it, Ben. We need unity, not division, right now, or we'll all find ourselves out of a job.'

'I'm going to apply for a transfer,' said Ben. 'I can't stand A Wing much longer.'

'So the rats are deserting . . .' said Brand sarcastically. 'You know you won't apply. The money's too good and you need it. Ben, with your standard of living.'

'Got a yacht, have you?' asked Boyd.

'Just an interest in cars. Like the vintage variety,' replied Ben. 'Ted's right – I'm only threatening. I *do* need the money.'

'What's the general view about the treatment of prisoners here?' asked Boyd.

'That it's too cushy,' said Brand.

'Rhodes seems harmless.' Boyd felt oddly protective.

'He *has* to go. I want him transferred.'

'Will he be allowed his books and papers in Broadmoor?'

'Maybe. That'll be down to the regime.'

'If he had to stop his work. I think he'd die.'

Ben suddenly sounded impatient. 'And let's leave it at that.'

'But what about the other inmates?' asked Boyd.

'I think our regime is right for them. I believe in it, or I wouldn't be working here, and I admire Neil Hathaway as a man and as a real visionary. Some lifers will never come out. But what are we going to do with them? What are they going to do with themselves? There must be a constructive regime. We can't lock 'em up every day while they go stir crazy.'

'That's not what the media thinks. Most of the tabloids are baying for retribution.'

'And so is the general public,' continued Brand. 'So our chances of closure are pretty high. I'm just living day to day. The announcement may come at any time. And we're getting hell from the other screws.'

'How's that?' asked Boyd.

'They think our regime is bringing Aston into disrepute just when its act got cleaned up. Most people here want lifers to be in another prison – or even in a unit that's much more isolated and independent.'

'Couldn't we survive that way?' asked Boyd.

'Too expensive.' Brand sounded dour and defeated.

'We could always take industrial action,' said Ben Maxwell.

'That would make a change.' Brand laughed and the tension eased. 'Industrial action to save something, rather than destroy it.'

But Boyd was hardly listening as he saw Mick Raymond, another of the officers from the unit, bearing down on them, disbelief in his eyes.

'What the matter with him?' asked Boyd uneasily. But he knew, and so did Brand. A feel of real dread crept over him, like a cold finger stirring in the pit of his stomach. Raymond was the winged messenger, the bringer of tidings. Bad tidings.

Chapter Eight

HM Prison Aston
22 June 2001 – 1315 hours

'What is it, Mick?' Brand had got to his feet and his hands were beginning to shake. A little pulse beat in his temple.

Gradually the canteen fell completely silent.

You don't have to say it, Boyd was thinking. You don't have to say it's happened again.

'Who?' Ben Maxwell's voice was expressionless.

'Parker. He's – I found him in the toilet. His throat's been cut.'

There was a buzz of conversation, a chatter that quickly came to a close.

'But how? I've had officers on the shutters. No one could have got in. No one. Where's Rhodes?' Brand was clearly beginning to lose control.

'In his pod. Working. He was on the monitor screens – all the time. He couldn't have left his pod. Who the fuck is doing this?' Mick Raymond stared at them all hopelessly. 'And how?'

'Is there any other way in?'

'No. The pods are completely secure.'

'This will finish us,' said Brand with conviction. He looked round at the silent prison officers at the tables, their meals abandoned. 'All right,' Brand yelled at them.

'You've had your fun. Eat, for fuck's sake, and I hope each mouthful chokes you.'

Brand, Maxwell and Boyd got up together and began to hurry out of the canteen, watched by the other officers. The silence was increasingly oppressive.

'He's been dead about an hour,' said the doctor.

Parker was sitting on the toilet, his trousers around his ankles. The gash across his throat had stopped pumping blood and had congealed in a hard, dark red crust. The bathroom floor was covered in gore.

In the pod's living space, the TV was playing a Bugs Bunny cartoon. Surely someone could turn it off, thought Boyd. But no one seemed able to take the initiative and the high-pitched voices and music continued to play while Parker's dead eyes still stared ahead. Blood had shot up over the basin and the magazine he had been reading was also liberally blood-soaked. The open page showed a male torso.

'Is this the same?' asked Boyd.

'Exactly,' replied Brand. 'A carbon copy of the other two. How the fuck did it happen? Who was watching the monitors?' He seemed beaten, incredulous and furious all at the same time.

'Banks and Hilton,' said Raymond. 'All the time. There was no way anyone was in this pod – except for Parker.'

'Then he got killed by the fairies,' said Brand. 'Is that a possibility?'

Before the police arrived, the doctor said, 'Don't touch anything. I've examined the body and I'll leave the rest to the forensic team.'

Brand nodded. 'I know the procedure.' He stared at Solly Parker's corpse with bitterness, almost as if Parker was personally responsible or had been deliberately careless.

91

'The screen blanked out,' said Hilton. 'But only for a very short period.'

'How short?' demanded Brand.

'Maybe a few seconds.'

'Not long enough to kill him.'

'Nowhere near.'

'Someone pulled the plug?' Boyd still couldn't work out what had happened.

'He was on camera,' said Hilton. 'He was watching TV, and then he went to the toilet. Then the screens went blank. But of course the toilet area isn't monitored.'

'How did the killer get in?'

'I don't know.' Hilton seemed to be in shock. 'There was no request for a laser key.'

'*How* did they get in?' Brand was determined that someone was going to tell him. But as the pod filled with an increasing number of prison officers, no one did.

'Maybe the killer was concealed in there for some time,' suggested Boyd. He reached up and clicked open one of the many small air-conditioning grilles, but there was only a minimum gauge ducting channel behind the plastic.

'How?' Brand was working himself into a rage. 'We should have insisted on installing cameras in the toilets. They've been watched masturbating – so what's the problem with watching them shitting?'

'The governor –' began one of the officers.

'Fuck the governor!' yelled Brand. 'He's done for now. And so are we.'

DI Lennox saw Boyd in a small, scruffy interview room in the main block that seemed to have escaped Hathaway's refurbishment – an isolated example of the original Aston. Lennox was young and well groomed, with an aggressive manner.

Boyd had no idea whether Lennox knew about his

identity or not, but was prepared to go through the interview under his alias.

DI Lennox began, however, with a particularly awkward question. 'What I can't understand is how you came into a prison for the first time in your life and were immediately placed in a high security unit without any experience at all.'

'I was in the army. That would have helped.'

'The inmates are violent criminals.'

'Yes.'

'Being a tough nut isn't enough. You would still need experience.'

'No one will work on the satellite.'

'It's highly paid.'

'But dangerous. As you can now understand.'

'You knew Parker?'

'Not really. I tried to avoid him.'

'Why?'

'He was a very predatory homosexual.'

'Did he make overtures to you?'

'Not exactly. But I caught the drift.'

'Did you feel threatened by him?'

'No.'

'Repulsed?'

'He was a rather repulsive man but that has nothing to do with being gay.'

'Which prisoner did you associate with most?'

'Rhodes.'

'He's a bit of a weirdo, isn't he?'

'Yes.'

'Do you consider him sane?'

'No.'

'Shouldn't he be in a psychiatric unit?'

'In my opinion, yes. But you'd have to ask the governor about that.'

'There seems to be a fine balance between insanity and sanity with these men.'

'Yes.'

'Do you agree with the principles behind this new unit?'

'I agree that the inmates, despite what they've done, should be treated as human beings and use their captivity as productively as the conditions of their detention permit.'

'You sound as if you're quoting from a manual.'

'I haven't had much time to read the manuals.'

'These killings – how do you account for them taking place in a top security unit with CCTV cameras everywhere and a large staffing complement?'

'I have a theory.'

'Which is?'

'I expect you'll have heard this already from Mr Brand.'

'Tell me in your own words.'

'We know whoever killed Jones, Royston and Parker somehow got into their pods and murdered them in the bathroom area where there's no camera.'

'And why *is* there no camera?'

'Because the governor has always been insistent that the lifers should retain their dignity. But in actual fact there's no need for a camera in the toilet area. No one can get into the pod because of the steel shuttering, and if they did they would be bound to be seen entering or leaving on the monitoring screens.'

'Have you any idea how someone could have got into the pod some other way?'

'I've looked at the original plans,' said Boyd. 'They're in the control room. I've even checked out the air-conditioning grilles. There's several of them in each pod, but they're minimum size – as is the actual ducting.'

'It's a total disaster,' said Lennox.

'I think there's been a deliberate attempt to close the wing and disgrace the governor.'

'Who by?' Lennox was watching Boyd very closely.

'Could be someone high up.'

'Do you mean someone on the management at Aston?'

'Possibly.'

'That sounds like paranoia.'

'I disagree. I think it's a possibility.'

'You're saying that you believe in a conspiracy to close the unit and get rid of the governor by murdering three inmates and making a mockery of the security system.'

Boyd shrugged, still wondering what Lennox knew about him.

Lennox looked round, got up, opened the door, checked the corridor, closed the door again and then searched the squalid little room in some detail. Satisfied, he turned back to Boyd and said, 'Well?'

'Were you looking for someone? Something?'

'I don't want to be overheard.'

'You're satisfied?'

'That there aren't any bugs? Yes, I *am* satisfied, Mr Boyd.'

'So you did know.'

'I've known all along.'

'Why didn't you say so then?'

'I thought I'd string you along. Just checking.'

'That I'm any good?'

'That sort of thing. So you believe in the conspiracy theory?' Lennox seemed slightly mocking.

'I can't think of another reason. Yet. What about you?'

Lennox shrugged. 'I'm only just catching up.'

'Is the governor going to resign?'

'Yes. He's going to be replaced by his PA, Angela Mason.'

'That's a strange choice.'

'Mason has been more or less filling the post of deputy governor. So she's rather more than a PA.'

'And what does *she* believe?'

'Angela Mason believes the unit should be closed.'

'She was never sold on the idea?'

'She didn't think A Wing was going to work – and now she's sure.'

'On what grounds?'

'Security – and an over-liberal regime.'

'What about the remaining inmates?'

'Jordan is going to Basildon.'

'What kind of set-up is Basildon?'

'Lock-up. No privileges.'

'And Rhodes?'

'He's being transferred to Broadmoor – on the doctor's recommendation.'

'Can that be done if the jury originally found him sane?'

'If his condition has deteriorated sufficiently.'

'So this is the death of an intelligent experiment.'

'Three down,' said Lennox. 'Two to go.'

'There won't be any more killings,' said Boyd. 'Surely the objective has been attained.'

'If closure *is* the objective.' Lennox sounded sceptical. 'Don't you have any other theories?'

'No,' snapped Boyd.

'Of course the wing has been a thorn in the side of the law and order brigade, and I can see they might well want to discredit Hathaway. But it would require enormous organisation to bring off three murders in these circumstances. It would *have* to be an inside job for a start.'

'I've believed that all along,' said Boyd. 'The point is – what kind of inside job? And how many staff are involved?'

Lennox paused and then said, 'If an outside group did want to close down A Wing, they'd have to infiltrate some of their own people well before they could kill three inmates on three separate occasions in a top security unit.'

'Don't underestimate the power of money,' said Boyd.

Lennox sighed. 'What about belief?'

Boyd said nothing, his mind racing back over old ground.

Lennox got up. 'You'll obviously contact me if you come up with any proof of infiltration?'

'And you'll do the same for me?'

'Of course.'

Boyd went towards the door.

'Before you go there's one other question: is there reason to suppose Rhodes is involved?'

'He's got an alibi. The staff will back that up – and so will the cameras.'

'How disappointing,' said Lennox. 'I'd so much rather have a mad crusader than all the complications of organised insiders.'

'I got in easily enough,' said Boyd. 'So why shouldn't anyone else? The job's highly paid but unpopular. I see A Wing as a comfortable nest for vipers. Don't you?'

'I'm beginning to think that way,' said Lennox unwillingly.

Boyd arrived back in A Wing at just after three.

'The governor wants to see you again,' said Brand. 'Or shall we say the ex-governor? He seems to have taken a shine to you.'

'Why?'

'I think he wants to talk to you about Rhodes – since you got on with him so well and Farley's away.'

'I'm only Farley's stand-in.' Boyd felt immediately anxious. Why should Hathaway send for a junior officer? Hadn't Brand been consulted?

'Or shall we say stooge? Anyway, Hathaway's trying to make up his mind about having Rhodes transferred to Broadmoor. But he'll need to be certified insane first. I've already seen Hathaway and told him I agree with the certification. But he seems to want to talk to you as well. Not bad for a second day.'

'I haven't had time to form any convictions about Rhodes.' Boyd could already hear warning bells.

'Maybe he thinks Broadmoor's a better way out for Rhodes. If he goes to Basildon, his research wouldn't be allowed. So Hathaway's humane to the last. Or should I just dismiss him as an idealist?'

'Most people have,' said Boyd.

Boyd knocked on the governor's door for the second time that day. He was conscious that he was being singled out far too much and Hathaway could be blowing his cover.

'Come in.'

Angela Mason was nowhere to be seen and Hathaway had a look of weary acceptance. He gestured to Boyd to follow him into the inner office where they had talked before. 'I've checked out the room again and there aren't any bugs.'

'You're really sure of that? Everything I'm doing could be blown away if there's yet another security breach.'

Hathaway went to the TV set and switched it on, turning up the sound on a games show. Then he sat down at his desk. He looked devastated, and Boyd pulled up a chair beside him.

'I know I'm taking a risk by calling you in again, but I've already seen Brand. My excuse for sending for you is that you've been seeing a lot of Rhodes. Do you think he's linked to these killings?'

'There's irrefutable CCTV evidence that he's in the clear.'

'Yes – so Brand tells me.'

'But you don't believe him?'

'I don't know who to believe – or what to believe. The whole business is like some appalling, never-ending nightmare. I hoped you might just have found some way he could have committed the murders.'

Hathaway paused, but Boyd was silent.

'If Rhodes is transferred to Basildon, he'll be banged up most of the time, and they certainly won't co-operate on research material and there'd be no question of prison officers running errands for him.'

'And Broadmoor?'

'If he's officially diagnosed insane then they'll regard his research as therapy. But I'm sure he won't meet anyone as benignly co-operative as Farley.'

'But at least he can continue with his project at Broadmoor?'

'I'm sure he will.'

'When did you officially resign?'

'I've got a press conference in an hour.'

Boyd paused for he had just had an idea. A very dangerous idea.

'Can I sit in on it?'

'That's too risky.' Hathaway was immediately alarmed. 'This meeting isn't very sensible either. But we have what you might call a time problem.'

'I'd like to draw their fire. Maybe I could be seen as a passionate believer in the ethos of A Wing?'

'After two days?' Hathaway was incredulous.

'Why not?'

'There are dozens of officers who've been on A Wing since its inception.'

'I'd still like to be there.'

'You're risking a chance of exposure.'

'I know,' said Boyd. 'But time's running out on me.'

'How does that justify exposure?'

Boyd hesitated and then said. 'It's the only way I can think of getting a reaction – pulling them out of the woodwork.'

'You could make yourself a sitting target.'

'That's the idea.' Boyd thought of Marcia and what could have been their future.

But he also knew he had no other choice. He was still a professional and this was the worst case he'd ever experienced. Boyd couldn't bring himself to end on such a bum note. If Marcia could be trusted – and he reckoned she could – this would definitely be his last case. He didn't want to go out in a blaze of glory, but not with a whimper either. He remembered the inscription on the sundial in Farley's garden. IT'S LATER THAN YOU

99

THINK. The phrase was relevant to almost everything that had happened at Aston so far.

'Unless someone exposes themselves – and they just might if they guess who I am – I don't see this case being cleared up in the very limited time we've got. Do you?'

'You might as well make a formal announcement.'

Boyd laughed and once again saw Marcia in his mind's eye.

'You think your appearance at this press conference could flush them out?' asked Hathaway.

'It's about my only chance.'

'You're a brave man, Mr Boyd,' said Hathaway. 'But you could be a very dead man too.'

'That's the risk I run.'

'I'll have to ask Brand to come as well.'

'Why not?'

'Very well.' Hathaway frowned. 'I have to say that I've never seen eye to eye with Brand, and I don't see him as a supporter. But I hope he'll be careful in front of the press.'

'I didn't realise you didn't get on with him,' said Boyd with surprise.

'He was always against the unit.'

'He didn't give me that impression. Brand seemed to be behind the entire philosophy. So why was he lying?'

'I was misguided enough to think he'd change his mind, but he told some civil servants the wing wasn't working – and he also complained to my deputy, Angela Mason. As you may know, she's no longer my deputy. She's my successor.'

'Is she against the unit too?'

'She's been persuaded.'

'By Brand?'

'Possibly. Anyway, she's going to close A Wing, so I'm afraid you'll soon be out of a job.'

'How long will she keep the wing open?'

100

'Only until Rhodes and Jordan have been transferred.'

'That justifies the risk I'm taking.'

Hathaway didn't reply.

'What's Angela Mason like?' asked Boyd anxiously.

'She has a lot of experience in the prison service and she worked here for over a year in a very senior position. She'll be well qualified to take over.'

'Are you sure she's totally against the unit?'

'I think she realises the wing was too much of a red-hot potato. Until the refurbishment, Aston had a bad history, and now its reputation will be even worse.' Hathaway got to his feet. 'As I said, I think you're a brave man to draw their fire. Remember how powerful they are. In other words, watch out for your own throat.'

But Boyd could only think of Marcia and the future they had promised each other. Why was he taking the risk of destroying all that? Did he still have a death wish? Or just a desire to end his career while he was still winning?

An hour later, the conference room of HM Prison Aston was packed with journalists, photographers and TV cameras. The lights in the long, newly decorated area enhanced the dark lustre of the table where Neil Hathaway and Angela Mason sat with Brand and Boyd to their right.

Boyd looked round him, sure now that he was the object of the attention of the other insiders who had worked so hard to bring about Hathaway's downfall and the closure of A Wing.

Hathaway read from a prepared statement. 'Because of the appalling and so far unsolved murders in the lifers' unit on A Wing, I'm resigning as governor of Aston Prison with immediate effect. I shall be replaced by my colleague, Angela Mason.'

He sat down, and Mason rose to her feet to read from

another prepared statement. Her voice shook slightly and Boyd was unable to work out whether the emotion was genuine or laid on for the occasion.

'I'd like to say that I bitterly regret Mr Hathaway's resignation. I've worked with him for over a year now and I have enjoyed the experience immensely. Neil Hathaway has been a remarkably innovative governor and I'm as shocked and horrified as he is about the murders of three of our inmates, and welcome the news that the police investigation has been stepped up as a result of the latest tragic incident.'

She sat down again and the questions began.

'Ray Chatterton. Express Newspapers. Why don't we have the investigating officer here?'

Angela Mason took the question, while Neil Hathaway watched her, as if in friendly curiosity.

'Because DI Lennox is interviewing witnesses. He'll be calling a press conference when he has more to say.' Angela Mason remained standing, as if to underline the fact that she would be answering all remaining questions.

'Torrin Dowden. The *Guardian*. How could these prisoners, in a top security unit, be murdered, one after the other, in exactly the same way?'

'That's what we are trying to find out.'

'Doesn't that underline that security in A Wing is null and void?'

'Security has been badly broken three times.'

'So it's an inside job –'

'DI Lennox is carrying out the enquiry.'

'He should be here.'

'I'm afraid you'll have to put up with me.'

'Derek Sheffield. Times Newspapers. As a result of these killings, will you be making any alterations to security arrangements in the future?'

'Yes. I will.' Angela Mason stared ahead while Neil Hathaway still gazed up at her benignly.

'Ben Latimer. *Daily Telegraph*. These appalling murders

have been the worst events in our prison system for many years. Would you agree with that?'

'I would agree that they are appalling.'

'What changes are you making? The public need to know.'

'I shall be closing A Wing directly the two remaining inmates have been transferred to other prisons.'

There was an intake of breath and Boyd noticed that Hathaway was no longer looking at Angela Mason but was staring down at the table.

'So A Wing is being closed.'

'That's what I said.'

'Because it's been a failure?'

'Because we believe that with adaptations the unit would be more viable as a safe and secure place for young offenders.'

'And the lifers?'

'Rhodes and Jordan will be transferred to other establishments.'

'James Gilbert. *Independent*. The unit in question was especially constructed for lifers and the wing's only been open a year. Surely this means the initiative has been a failure? A Wing was opened with a press conference which most of us attended and I distinctly remember Mr Hathaway extolling the virtues of the new policy, and the new building. What exactly has gone so badly wrong?'

Angela Mason gazed down at Neil Hathaway who nodded slightly. She then sat down and he once again rose reluctantly to his feet.

'Yes,' he began. 'We started with great hope, and as you know the design of the unit is unique. Although we understood that we were housing men of considerable violence, you have to appreciate that, in many cases, life actually means life. There would be no parole due to the very nature of their crimes, and our role was to provide a constructive and purposeful place for these men to live, and we believe we were achieving that. But the fact that we still don't know how security was penetrated –

103

three times, despite considerable tightening – means that the system needs completely reassessing before we can be confident of viable security.'

'You're closing down,' the journalist continued. 'Not waiting for a revised security system?'

Hathaway paused. 'I'm afraid the Home Office have lost faith in the potential of A Wing and that was the reason for my resignation.'

'Because you failed?'

'Because there's been a major security failure. That's where the fault lies, and not in the philosophy of the system and the ethos of the environment itself.'

He sat down and Angela Mason rose to her feet again. 'I'd like to introduce you to Ted Brand, the prison officer in charge of the unit, and our latest recruit, Luke Taylor, an officer who only started his career with us a few days ago.'

Boyd and Brand now stood up. Brand looked self-conscious and Boyd wondered if he was a pawn in Angela Mason's game. Or someone else's.

'Can you tell us what went wrong?' asked one of the television reporters.

Brand looked expressionlessly back at the camera. 'We had major security breaches and I've still no idea how they occurred.'

'Do you think prison officers were involved?'

'They've all been extensively vetted, so I think that's most unlikely.'

'The officers may have been vetted, but surely the killer would have found it hard to operate without co-operation or even extraordinary carelessness on their part? And the killer is still at large.'

'I can assure you that we have redoubled precautions and I'm responsible for the safety of the remaining two inmates – Jon Jordan and William Rhodes – until they are transferred to other institutions.'

'Did you really believe in such a liberal environment for these highly dangerous men?'

There was a long pause and then Brand began to

speak again, this time much more slowly. 'I have to say I had initial doubts about the system, which I *did* find too liberal for a regime involving lifers.'

Bullshit, thought Boyd. Brand was clearly protecting himself.

'Yet you took on the job.'

'At first I thought that the system *would* be more productive. But two of the inmates indulged in a homosexual relationship and another was deeply disturbed and should not have been in the unit. I'm afraid that for me the regime I had to manage didn't feel right. I'm a simple law and order man myself and there's no more to be said.'

Bullshit, thought Boyd yet again.

As he talked, Neil Hathaway watched Brand almost fearfully. Don't give yourself away, thought Boyd. Then he realised that he had calculatedly given himself away completely.

'Well, Mr Taylor,' asked another TV reporter. 'Are you a believer?'

'Very much so.' Boyd was crisp although he could mentally see his image flickering from millions of TV screens, asking someone to recognise him for the imposter he was and try to eliminate him. But that was the risk he'd taken. There was no other way. If he survived, this *had* to be his last job. 'I thought the unit had great potential and although there have clearly been the most disastrous security breaches, the experiment *was* proving successful. It was the security problems that wrecked any chances of survival.'

'Why do you think the unit had potential?'

'Because the policy was humane and treated lifers decently. As far as I can tell, there was no weakness in the way the men were treated – only encouragement to lead a positive and productive way of life. And I think that's right.'

Hathaway permitted himself a small smile of satisfaction. Brand looked slightly rattled, and Angela Mason sighed gently, but loudly enough to make her point.

105

'Who do you think killed those men?'

'I don't know.'

'Do *you* think prison officers could have been bribed?'

'It's possible.'

Ted Brand gave Boyd an admonishing look, as if he had spoken out of turn.

'Do you personally know of any instance when an officer has been bribed?'

'No.'

'Do you think another inmate carried out the murders?'

'No. I think it's more likely to be an outsider.'

'Helped by a prison officer?'

Boyd shrugged and watched with some satisfaction the look of studied objectivity disappear from Angela Mason's face.

Then another reporter stood up and said, 'This is all very well, Mr Taylor, but how can we have any faith in what you're saying when you've only spent a couple of days on A Wing? We should be talking to a much more established officer.'

'That's true,' said Boyd. 'No one else volunteered.'

'Which says it all.' The reporter sat down.

Boyd waited with Brand as the press were shown out of the conference room by a group of prison officers while Hathaway and Mason appeared to be talking amicably.

'You blew it.' Brand was furious. 'Why did you give them that shit?'

'Because I believe in that shit. Because I believe in Hathaway's system – and I thought you did too. That's what you led me to believe anyway.'

Brand looked flustered and Boyd enjoyed his discomfort.

'I'm afraid I got disillusioned.'

'Then you should have said so – and left.'

'Don't damn well tell me what to do!'

'I'm not. It's up to your conscience.'

Boyd was surprised by the anger in Brand's eyes.

'I'm going to get you transferred to another part of Aston,' said Brand. 'As from now.'

Boyd realised that he'd been so preoccupied with the risk he'd been running that he had forgotten the other repercussions. Now Brand was going to put him out of operation and a wave of panic filled him.

'You can't do that.'

'I can do what I like. I'm still in charge of A Wing and I can hire and fire as I please.' He leant over to Angela Mason, interrupting her conversation with Hathaway. Brand muttered something to her and she looked at her watch.

'I'd like to see you in my office right away, Mr Taylor,' she said crisply.

'Why's that, Angela?' asked Hathaway and for a moment she hesitated.

'You do realise you should be clearing your desk, Neil,' she said gently.

But Hathaway simply repeated the question. 'Why's that, Angela? What are you going to say to Mr Taylor?'

'Please, Neil. Don't let's end up like this.'

'Like what? I simply want to know what you're going to say to him.'

'I should have thought that was obvious.'

'You mean you're going to sack Mr Taylor, simply because he believes in the new unit – and all A Wing stands for?'

'As you know, the unit is being closed.'

'And are you sacking Mr Taylor?'

Angela Mason stood up and began to walk away.

'Are you sacking him, Angela? Do tell.'

A group of prison officers turned to stare at Hathaway as the TV crews dismantled their equipment.

He turned to Boyd with a shrug. 'She's not communicating well, is she?'

'So I'm going to be fired?'

107

'Possibly.'

'For believing in the system.'

'I'm sorry.' For a moment their eyes met and Boyd could see Hathaway's acute disappointment.

Then he had a sudden idea. 'I'd better tell her who I am,' whispered Boyd.

'You can't do that.' Hathaway was immediately agitated.

'Why not?'

'I don't trust her.'

Boyd thought hard. 'I've got to tell her sometime.'

'Not yet.' Hathaway was pleading. 'Let everything settle down. Let her think you're just a believer. She won't sack you completely – you're too good for that. Don't you think you might influence other officers? And what about Farley when he gets back? Drag Angela Mason into our confidence now and you really will have blown it.'

'I did that when I asked to come to this conference.'

'No.' Hathaway was insistent. 'You tried to flush them out. We have to wait and see if they show their hand. To involve Angela would be a great mistake. I'm sure it would.'

Boyd felt the fear and anxiety move inside him, a hard nugget now, a realisation of how alone he was, bearing the weight of so many expectations. Even Hathaway was ignoring him now, scribbling on a piece of paper.

'This is my mobile number. I'd appreciate you keeping in touch.'

Boyd was sitting opposite Angela Mason in the governor's office.

'I'm sorry you feel the way you do, Mr Taylor.' She seemed relaxed and confident.

'Do you want me to apologise for speaking out of turn?'

'No. And you wouldn't anyway.' She gave him a sad smile. 'I just happen to disagree with you.'

'Did you publicly disagree with Mr Hathaway?'

'Not publicly.'

'Or privately?'

'No.'

'Wouldn't that have been a good idea?'

'Are you telling me how to do my job?' For the first time she was defensive.

'No. I hate being leant on, that's all.'

'Who's leaning on you?'

'Isn't that what you're doing right now?' Boyd looked round for Brand, half expecting him to suddenly emerge from some inner sanctum.

'I feel that unity is important. Especially at a time like this. We shouldn't be seen to be split. Not the governor, nor a junior employee who's had no experience at all of prison systems. I really can't imagine why Mr Brand employed you.'

Boyd wondered if she was deliberately playing games. Could she have always known who he was? The thought troubled him deeply.

'I think he may have seen some qualities in me, and I wanted the job.' Boyd paused. 'Can I ask you a question? There's something I really don't understand – something about you and Mr Brand.'

'Of course.' She looked at him curiously.

'As you were both working with Mr Hathaway on a new project, why didn't you discuss your doubts with him?'

'I would have thought that was obvious.'

'Not to me.'

'Once these terrible killings began, once security had been so badly breached, I knew – and I'm sure Mr Brand knew too – that the situation had run out of control.'

'Is that all? You're talking about intervention – not the ethos of the unit.'

Angela Mason was silent for a moment and he wondered if she was about to close the discussion. Then she said, 'Security problems and dangerous criminals don't mix. Once the unit hit the headlines, the experiment was over. Surely you realise that? The public has a right to know that a regime – however humane – is completely secure. So it wasn't a question of not believing in the aim. It was to do with how that aim was achieved. Now I'm of the opinion that the unit had a fatal flaw from inception. The security system could be penetrated.'

Why is she talking to me like this? Boyd wondered. I'm an unimportant, new warder who made an idealistic speech at the wrong time. But wasn't *that* the very reason?

'Events crept up on us.' Angela Mason was still very calm and there was no trace of hesitation in her voice. 'Both Mr Brand and I began sharing a full belief in Mr Hathaway's experiment. But there were other factors before security became such a problem. The homosexual activity, Rhodes's book and the fact that Farley had become his research assistant. Doesn't the regime seem a little lax?'

'As far as I'm concerned, the inmates were recognised as human beings and allowed dignity.'

'Rhodes is insane.'

'He wasn't found insane by the jury.'

'There's no point in arguing. As far as I'm concerned, you're off the unit,' Mason said dismissively. 'I'll get Brand to place you in another part of Aston.'

'All for speaking my mind?'

'You're very inexperienced. You've never worked for the prison service before.'

'So my views are discounted?' There was irony in Boyd's voice.

'You need more experience,' Angela Mason insisted. 'And you're lucky not to be dismissed.'

Thank God I didn't try to confide in her, thought Boyd. I would have lost everything.

Back on A Wing, Brand was briefing a new shift while those still on duty from the previous one gazed at the CCTV monitors. The surviving inmates were in predictable mode, with Rhodes writing vigorously, and Jordan watching television lethargically, lying on his bed.

Boyd gazed at the two shifts reflectively, wondering yet again if there could be a group within a group, some kind of pre-arranged cell dedicated to closing A Wing in the most cold-blooded way imaginable. The whole notion now seemed to have the ring of a TV series on a low budget. But how else could the killings have been carried out?

The atmosphere grew more tense as Brand turned away from his briefing to view Boyd with displeasure.

'You've been transferred to C Wing,' he said brusquely. 'You should be there now.'

'I just wanted to know what I was taking on,' replied Boyd, allowing his indignation to show.

'They're a mixed bag of recidivists. They know Aston better than almost anyone.'

'I'd prefer to work here. I'm meant to be helping Rhodes.' Boyd knew that his plea was only a gesture.

'That's over. Go to C Wing.' Brand paused. 'In fact, I'll have someone take you over now. Don – please take Mr Taylor to Colin Drake.'

'OK.' Don Gibson was middle-aged with a spreading waistline and lank hair with a centre parting. Boyd had not seen him before. 'Let's get down there. We've a lot to do before we can shut this unit down.'

Boyd and Gibson crossed the concrete strip that led to the main buildings and walked down a long corridor which passed the kitchens. There was a smell of roasting beef.

'I can't take this place much longer,' said Gibson. 'I'm leaving to work in my brother's off-licence which means a huge drop in salary, but at least I'll be out of here.'

Boyd was taken aback. Why should Brand have chosen Gibson to be his guide? Why place him with another dissident? Then Boyd began to wonder if Brand could possibly have made the decision intentionally.

'I can see how the place would get to you.'

'How long do you really intend staying?'

'I don't know. I'm very disappointed at being moved out of A Wing.'

'You didn't follow the party line.'

'Maybe I don't know what the party line is. All I did was to honestly say what I felt. I didn't realise the extent of the animosity.'

'Who says there is any?'

'That's the way it feels.'

'The unit just couldn't survive those killings. In all my time as a prison officer I've never seen anything like it. I still can't believe they happened.'

'There seem to be various theories,' said Boyd cautiously. 'But in my opinion none of them really add up.'

'Whatever happens, there must have been an insider – someone who's still operating – and maybe more than one.'

'I reckon it's possible there are more insiders than you think.' Boyd realised all too well the ironic ambiguity of what he was saying. But, leaving himself out of it, could a shift have been penetrated? If so, the infiltrators must have been recruited a long time ago and slowly put in place. But even if that was the case, different shifts had been on duty at the times of the killings. So to have insiders only on one shift wouldn't have made any sense at all. But suppose *each* shift had been slowly infiltrated? Taken at first glance the idea seemed ludicrous. But over a period of time it was possible. Just possible.

Boyd decided to try out his theory on his companion and when they came to a series of what seemed to be interview rooms, he paused, opened a door and beckoned Gibson inside. He was about to take yet another risk, but at least he reckoned he had logic on his side. Here was the recently established, earnest young prison officer, relieved of his duties because of his belief in the failed system, hoping to recruit other dissenters. Surely no one could quarrel with that?

'Can we talk for a moment?'

Gibson looked at his watch. 'I haven't got much time. Ted will need —'

'We've got a few minutes.'

'OK.'

They entered the dusty little room that didn't seem to have been used for a long time. There were piles of requisition forms in a corner and a stack of outdated telephone books.

'How many warders to a shift?'

'You should know that — there are eight.'

'But you've been short-staffed —'

'Sure. But there are never less than six, and, anyway, the same shift wasn't on duty during each of the killings. There must have been at least two involved.'

Boyd decided to test his theory. 'OK, so each time the whole shift was infiltrated.'

'How do you mean?' Gibson looked at him as if he had suddenly taken leave of his senses.

Boyd spoke quietly and he hoped with considerable conviction. 'Let's say long-term insiders had been planted when the unit first opened, and were scattered through the shifts.'

'With a view to what?'

'With a view to wrecking the credibility of the unit at the right moment.'

'They would have had to hang around for a long time — a year in fact.'

'Don't insiders always have to play a waiting game?' said Boyd. 'And they could be collecting two salaries,' he added quickly. 'High salaries. The official and the unofficial.'

'But most of the officers came from other departments. Some of them have been working at Aston for a very long time.'

'Suppose those departments had been infiltrated with the objective of ultimately building up a cell?'

'What about the time span?'

'How long had the unit been planned?'

'Some years. It was Hathaway of course who set A Wing in motion.' Gibson suddenly seemed much more interested in Boyd's hypothesis. 'But what about recruitment? A Wing officers are selected by Brand himself.'

'That's interesting.'

'You mean you think Brand's in on it? But why? Why should someone go to all this trouble? Just to make a political point? OK – so the unit's being closed because of the killings. Big deal.'

'Suppose A Wing had been a success?' said Boyd. 'Identical facilities could be set up in other prisons.'

'Why should that matter so much? Well, all right, I can see it could matter in some quarters, but a lot of people agree with all you said at that press conference – even if you did get the order of the boot.'

'From Brand.'

Gibson didn't say anything for a while. Then he repeated, 'Yes – the order of the boot from Brand.'

There was a long silence during which Boyd's thoughts raced. He was proposing a conspiracy and a long-term infiltration. Could this really have been put in place? Well, the IRA managed to do it, so why shouldn't someone else have a go? Regular implants over a period of time, highly paid and with the promise of great rewards. And then the killings. Boyd felt a rush of adrenalin, particularly when he saw the acceptance in Gibson's eyes.

'What *about* Brand?' asked Boyd. 'Could he have set this up, put the long, slow operation in motion?'

'It's too far fetched.' Don Gibson looked uneasy. 'I mean, for Christ's sake . . .' His voice petered out. Then he said hesitantly, 'Over a period, perhaps . . .'

'And maybe the killings are just a beginning,' prompted Boyd.

'You mean, all this could have been just a rehearsal for some bigger project?' Gibson was looking at Boyd in consternation.

114

Boyd was relieved and disappointed at the same time. He had wanted to sow the seeds, flag information so that he might gather more. It didn't look as if these tactics were going to pay off with Don Gibson, but on the other hand, Gibson might be a member of the cell himself. Either way, Boyd knew he had to press on and take the risk.

'It's possible.'

'Brand?'

'I'm not saying that Brand is involved. But the operation would be very smooth-working if he was. Who advises Brand on recruitment?'

'God knows.' Gibson looked at him blankly. 'I honestly feel you're jumping to conclusions – and pretty ludicrous conclusions at that.'

But Boyd could see he was worried and his imagination raced ahead. Could there be other targets? First, destruction of A Wing. Then what? Some kind of break-out? A spreading cell in a high security prison system, carefully recruited and held on course, could have coils everywhere, and wide-ranging objectives. Sounding an alert could bring swift action aimed at himself – but only if Gibson was involved. Boyd didn't think much time would elapse before he knew, and his own personal fear began to grow, getting in the way of all logical thought, scrambling his mind.

'I'd better get on,' said Gibson.

But what with? wondered Boyd.

'Nice and easy does it,' said Colin Drake, the senior officer in C Wing as he and Boyd sat in his cramped office with an old-fashioned girlie calendar and bile green carpet.

Colin Drake was a youngish man with a blue jowl, freckles and a slightly over-assertive manner which inadequately concealed his cynicism.

'We house the old lags, the recidivists. Men who've

115

been institutionalised for years and find life too hard outside Aston.'

'The majority are reoffenders?'

'Yes.'

'So they're happier here?'

'They moan and complain, but settle back in fairly quickly. It's a way of life that we provide. Of course there are exceptions to the rule. Some of them can't handle captivity at all – not in their early days anyway, and that's when the prison officers have to be counsellors as well as figures of authority.' Drake paused. 'Haven't you been counselling Rhodes?'

'I was his errand boy.'

'Is that a criticism of the A Wing regime?'

Boyd realised he'd given the wrong impression. 'I meant that I changed his library books for him.'

'At the taxpayer's expense?'

'Mine. I had to pay a fine.'

'Well – if you will work for a liberal regime –'

'Do you think it was liberal?'

'There's a good idea lurking somewhere,' said Drake. 'But it didn't get out. You did, though.'

'I fell foul of Brand.'

'Really?'

'I backed the liberal regime in a press conference.'

'What did you do that for?'

'Because I believed in the regime.'

'But how come you were called to a press conference when you'd only been on A Wing for a few hours?'

'Days, actually.'

'All the same. Whose idea was that?'

'Hathaway's.'

'What a prick.'

'Maybe.'

'Couldn't he have got someone with a slightly *longer* track record?' Drake was scoffing.

'Anyway – now I'm all yours.'

'What a thrill.' Then Drake relented. 'I hear you did well though.'

116

'Who did you hear that from?'

'Secret sources. Well, you'll find you're rushed off your feet down here. It's not like A Wing – killings on the hour every hour.' He laughed. 'I wonder if Jordan and Rhodes will make it out of there.'

C Wing was a far cry from the lifers' environment, with banks of cells, each floor linked by metal walkways, a vast gantry-like complex, a web of steel with a large association area inside and a much larger area outside with painted goal posts and a basketball court. The cells, designed for two inmates, were wide and roomy, with TV sets and an optional exercise bike as well as a barred window that overlooked an allotment.

During his afternoon duties, which involved a visual check on each cell and its inmates, Boyd got talking to an elderly recidivist by the name of Billy Barnes.

'You're new then.' Billy was sitting on his bed, reading an Agatha Christie novel which he put down, carefully flattened to keep his place.

'I was on A Wing.' Boyd was anxious to strike up a casual conversation to see how the grapevine had recorded the latest turn of events.

Billy Barnes's round, pug-like face lit up with pleasure. 'You must have seen all them corpses.'

'Just one.'

'We hear a massacre's got going over there. What price security now, eh?'

'The wing's closed.'

'As it should be. Fucking sloppy experiment. Lifers should get what they deserve.'

'And what's that?'

'Between them that bunch have notched up a blood bath,' said Billy. 'They should be doing hard grind, not hanging around in those pods doing sweet FA. Breaking up rocks – that's what they should be doing. If I had my way, they'd have been topped, not given the life of Riley.'

117

Boyd nodded, trying to appear sympathetic. 'A lot of people think that.'

'Look – I've spent half my life in here, one way and another. But all I done was forge credit cards. Now what's the harm in that?'

'Makes for a little confusion,' said Boyd.

'Confusion's nothing compared with what they done. I think they should've been given the chop.' Billy was anxious, however, to see what Boyd knew. 'How the hell could it have happened? Three of them topped in a few days.'

'What does the grapevine say?' asked Boyd.

'You got a right gang of bandits around.'

'What's that meant to mean?'

'What it says. It's got to be the screws, right?'

'You mean they were infiltrated?'

'Eh?'

'You mean some bent ones got planted?'

'Stands to reason, doesn't it?'

Once he was off duty, Boyd felt a curious combination of elation and despondency. Elation because the Aston grapevine clearly backed up his theory of infiltration, despondency because he didn't know what to do next.

When Boyd got back to the flat he decided to use his mobile to ring Hathaway, just in case his line had been tapped or the flat bugged. He had, of course, searched the place, but nowadays the bugs could be so high tech he could never be sure.

Boyd was feeling increasingly nervous. The realisation had always been at the back of his mind, but now it was very much at the fore. He was an insider against insiders, a group who were far stronger than he was. To get the fast results he needed, Boyd had deliberately exposed his alias to public scrutiny and that could mean only one thing. He was in their sights.

They could kill him as easily as the lifers.

Surely it was only a matter of time before they responded?

For a moment, Boyd wondered if he could have been wrong, that there was no ring of conspirators, no long-term recruited group of insiders. The three murders might have been committed in some other way; security might have been defeated by another ruse.

Boyd got out his mobile and looked up the number that Hathaway had given him.

'Neil Hathaway?'

'Speaking.'

'It's Boyd. Can I come and see you?'

'When?'

'Now?'

'Is there some new development?'

'Yes. How do I get to you?'

Hathaway gave him directions.

'I'll be with you as quickly as possible.'

'You sound intriguing.'

'The thing about intrigue,' said Boyd, 'is that you never know the extent.'

Chapter Nine

Carshalton, Surrey
22 June 2001 – 1845 hours

Neil Hathaway's house, Fernlea, was large and Victorian, set in a similar neighbourhood on what had once been wooded hills, now packed with infill maisonettes and on a fast dual carriageway. There was a lost feeling to Fernlea and its counterparts, as if they knew their world had been overtaken.

As he approached, to his concern, Boyd saw there were a large number of cars parked in the drive.

He went across to a heavy oak front door overhung with wisteria. He was about to knock when the door was opened by Hathaway himself. There were children shouting in one room and a noisy gaggle of adults in another.

'Am I interrupting something?' Boyd asked.

'Just a children's party.'

'We have to talk.'

'Come through.' Hathaway led Brand past a large sitting room that was full of people and into a small book-lined study with a desk piled high with papers. 'Do sit down,' Hathaway said, indicating a chair beside the desk.

Boyd did as he was told and Hathaway placed himself in a swivel office chair.

'Can I get you something?'

'No, thanks.'

Hathaway waved a hand at the paperwork on his

desk. 'I had to turn out this lot from my office at Aston.
I'll have to get something specially made for them.' He
paused. 'So what's the emergency?'

'I think Aston's been infiltrated over a number of
years by prison officers who are being paid to sabotage
the prison.'

'Who by?'

'That I don't know.'

'Is this rumour or –'

'Deduction. I obviously can't be certain.'

'And what's the point of the infiltration?' Hathaway
was watching Boyd with an air of scepticism.

'To undermine Aston on a variety of different levels.'

'I don't understand.'

'What I *think* has happened is that Aston was targeted
some years ago and the infiltrators were gradually put
in place. There could be a dozen of them – maybe
more.'

'The idea being to . . .'

'Make a series of fast strikes. The first one was to close
A Wing and secure your resignation.'

'Well, someone's certainly done that. So what's
next?'

'A riot. An escape. Maybe both.'

'And who do you reckon is behind all this?'

'The person or persons could be political – or
criminal.'

'Criminal?' Hathaway looked taken aback. 'You mean
that the infiltrators could be paid to spring certain
prisoners?'

'It could happen.'

'So the closure and my resignation are just the tip of
the iceberg?'

'Something like that.'

'Something like that is hard to believe.'

'Then how else do you explain these killings? For
them to go unobserved by cameras *and* staff? At least
two infiltrated shifts would have had to be involved.'

'Christ!' Hathaway was gazing intently at Boyd, his

scepticism on hold. 'To infiltrate two entire shifts – one of which was on duty twice – is really going some. Who would co-ordinate all this?'

'How about Brand?'

Hathaway gazed at him steadily. 'Isn't this conspiracy theory going well over the top?'

'It would make the impossible possible.'

There was a long silence between them.

Then Boyd said, 'If we look at the way the killings were accomplished – we don't have to have a totally infiltrated shift.'

'Tell me more.'

'If there are eight prison officers on a shift, you'd only need half of those men to be working for the enemy. Two could disable the cameras and make sure the log book made no mention of their failure, and the other two could carry out the murders. What's more, Brand would take care not to be on either of those shifts. He'd simply co-ordinate the duties of each infiltrator.'

Hathaway nodded. 'OK. But what about the other four? They would have noticed any camera cut-out.'

'Not if they were sufficiently distracted.'

'How?'

'I don't know.'

'And why was it so important to get me out?'

'Angela Mason?'

Hathaway looked shattered. 'What are the implications there?'

'That she's another implant.'

'She's been with us for just over a year. Before that she was deputy governor of Standen –'

'The women's prison?'

'And before Standen she was on the management team at Hatfield. She's got a degree in criminology and came into the service on a graduate trainee scheme.'

'Sounds good material.'

'She is. But that apart, the more I think about your conspiracy theory the more possible some of it seems.

And there's something else. We've got seven inmates at Aston who belong to the Maxton Syndicate.'

'What the hell's the Maxton Syndicate?'

'A highly sophisticated group of criminals, largely based in Manchester.'

'What are they doing time for?'

'Various forms of villainy, including forgery, protection, racketeering and money laundering. Sentences vary from twelve to fifteen years. The Syndicate might be arranging to spring them. Maybe what happened to A Wing, and to me, was simply an aperitif, a dummy run for the real McCoy.'

'But they'd only succeed in having syndicate members on the run.'

'Not if they had a total make-over. Plastic surgery and new identities.'

'Would they be worth this kind of trouble?'

'Definitely. I should have told you that two of them are the Maxton brothers themselves – James and Alistair. They're like junior Krays – but with a much bigger empire. They'd like to be operating again, even if they had to be outside the UK. Anyway, for Christ's sake, they'd want their freedom.'

Boyd nodded. 'And the Syndicate has plenty of money?'

'Absolutely.'

'And to have a co-ordinator would be essential.'

'I would imagine so. But for Angela Mason to be part of the Syndicate does seem a little unlikely. Why should she work for them?'

'Money.'

'She has a lot to lose.'

'Blackmail – but the trouble is,' Boyd admitted, 'conspiracy theories always suffer from imaginative overkill.'

'I thought you were sold on the idea,' said Hathaway.

'I'm sold on the infiltration, I'm sold on there being a co-ordinator, but the question is who? Brand at middle

123

management level, or Mason at the top of the tree?' Boyd paused and looked at Hathaway reflectively. 'Why wasn't she deputy governor? She'd been in that role before.'

'It wasn't in her job description at Aston.'

'Is there another deputy governor?' asked Boyd.

'No. There's a management team.'

'Which she's part of?'

'Very much so, but she wanted to specialise.'

'In what?'

'Education. She has this theory that Aston should produce a much more rounded education policy, and she wanted to develop that. I was all for it, but I also wanted to work very closely with her.'

'So she became your PA.'

'We were jointly responsible for the project. There were some delays, however, because I wanted to get A Wing off the ground first. The delays must have been frustrating for her.'

'In fact they probably weren't,' said Boyd. 'Not if she was working for the Maxton Syndicate.'

'Well, it couldn't have been for money. She's very highly paid by HM Prison Service.'

'So they have something on her, and if we *are* considering her seriously –'

'I'm not sure we are,' put in Hathaway.

'– then what *could* they have on her?'

'God knows.' Hathaway paused. 'Unless . . .'

'Unless what?' Boyd was impatient.

'She has a brother who's been in trouble with the law. I understand he was a pederast.'

'Did she talk about him?'

'Never. The information was in her confidential file.'

'Where is he?'

'He was in Linton – there's a wing there for sexual offenders. But he's been out for some years.'

'So where is he now?'

'Working in Coventry as an accountant at a bus company, according to the file. But I've never picked up the slightest hint of any stress, and if she wanted to protect her brother she could have come to me – or anyone else on the management team – for help. It's unlikely that she'd allow herself to be blackmailed by the Maxton Syndicate.'

Boyd had to agree. 'But at least there's some mileage in the infiltration theory.'

'I would say there's a lot of mileage in the idea, but how are you going to get hard evidence if they don't rise to your bait?'

'They will,' said Boyd. 'It's only a matter of time.'

'They could kill you.'

'There's always a drawback to role play.'

'And you're really prepared to run such a personal risk?'

Boyd pushed away the thought of Marcia. 'Programming my own destruction has always been high on the agenda in this kind of work. It's become a habit. And I want to bring all this to a speedy conclusion.'

'And yourself?'

'I'm used to ducking and diving.'

'I hope so.'

There was a pause.

'Isn't there some way you could get back into the unit?' said Hathaway. 'At least you'd be back in the thick of it.'

'Only by gambling on Angela Mason being in the clear and telling her who I am. I know you were against that, but I reckon it's got to be done.' Boyd got up. 'Is there anything else you can tell me?' he asked.

'I still think you'd be unwise to come clean with Angela.'

'I'll have to take the risk. After all, I've already put my head in the noose,' said Boyd.

'And you want someone to kick away the chair?'

Boyd drove back to the flat, let himself in and flopped down on the sofa, exhausted and emotionally drained.

Suddenly he decided to phone Lennox on his mobile. He tried Aston and then the station. Eventually he got hold of him. 'You're working late.'

'I need to.' He sounded as drained as Boyd felt.

'Any results?'

'Not yet.'

'I've just been to see Hathaway at his home and had an interesting discussion. But I've no evidence to back up the suggestion I made and which Hathaway seemed to find supportable.'

'Tell me the story.'

'Suppose infiltrators had been gradually employed as prison officers at Aston over a period of years? Suppose their salaries were augmented by retainers?'

'With a view to doing what?'

'With a view to undermining Aston completely, beginning with the closure of A Wing and Hathaway's resignation.'

Lennox sighed. 'I find it hard to believe in conspiracy theories.'

'Suppose the final step was to organise a break-out? A break-out that would include some high profile prisoners.'

'Like who?'

'The Maxton brothers.'

Lennox was silent.

'And you do realise that however slow the build-up was, the results would have to be achieved fast to be effective.'

'In a matter of days?'

'I would think so.'

'So the Trojan Horse has been activated?'

'You sound as if you still don't believe me.'

'On the contrary,' said Lennox. 'I'm beginning to think you've got a point.'

'Have you interviewed and checked the background of every officer on the unit?'

'Yes – and double-checked them.'

'Have you talked to the families?'

'Yes.'

'How many officers didn't have a family, were single, or divorced?'

There was the sound of rustling paper as Lennox consulted a printout. 'Seven.'

'Those are the officers you need to concentrate on.'

'OK. We'll look at them again.' Lennox was now slightly flustered. 'Tell me – would seven men have been able to undermine the system sufficiently to kill three times?'

'I think it's possible.'

'But they wouldn't be on one shift. I mean – how could they?'

'I'm not saying they were, but to achieve these killings each incident only needed to have a few infiltrators.'

'So that means we're looking for a co-ordinator.'

'How about Brand? To what extent have you been able to check him?'

'Pretty thoroughly. He has a wife and three kids, and his parents are still alive.' Lennox paused and then asked curiously. 'How did Hathaway take all this?'

'He was interested.'

'In his position I expect he wanted to believe you.'

'Yes. I accept that. I also wondered if Angela Mason could be involved.'

'For God's sake – how high up the ladder are you intending to go with your conspiracies? What about the Queen Mother?'

'I don't think she'd be a lot of use in this situation.'

'You tell me what is.'

'Suppose I go to Mason and tell her who I am, and ask to be reinstated?'

'I don't think you should do anything of the kind.' Lennox paused. 'I wonder if she guessed you were an insider. Those two meetings with Hathaway were a bit unlikely for a new prison officer with no experience.'

'I've had to run some obvious risks because of the time factor – but it's largely been useless. I've exposed nothing at all.'

'That's what they all say while they button up their long macs.'

Boyd laughed and then felt a sudden loss of confidence.

But Lennox, like Hathaway, seemed to have been won over. 'Your theory would account for killings that have always seemed technically impossible. And undermining the regime at Aston still further would certainly please the law and order lobby.' Lennox paused. 'But I still can't get over your involvement at the press conference.'

'I wanted to draw their fire.'

'That's not how you should be working,' said Lennox impatiently.

'On the contrary – it's the only way I *can* work.'

'If that's the way you feel, I think you *should* take another risk and get Mason to reinstate you. The dying hours of A Wing might hold the answer to all our prayers.'

'I'm out of the habit of praying,' said Boyd.

Chapter Ten

Boyd sat in his flat and stared down at the urban scene below him. The pavement still bustled with people heading for the bus station at the end of the road while others were walking away from it. The road had been pedestrianised and was closed to vehicles, except those delivering to shops. In the centre of what had once been a small square was a floodlit children's playground with a slide, a roundabout and a see-saw, all made of scuffed plastic. There were no children there, but sitting on the see-saw was a young man eating some sort of takeaway. Boyd continued to gaze down at the young man who seemed in no hurry, eating mechanically, as if the food was plastic.

Boyd's thoughts returned to the entirely plastic world of A Wing. Plastic and steel. Shiny surfaces glinting forbiddingly. Was the young man waiting for him to come down, to walk across the scrappy little square so that he could gun him down, or was there someone else concealed in the plastic world, ready to kill him from a vantage point? OK, so he'd asked for it, so wasn't that all he could expect?

Then Boyd remembered there was a rather good Chinese takeaway just around the corner and suddenly he had an insatiable appetite for the tang of sweet and sour prawns. He had to have comfort. He had to have comfort food. At the same time. Boyd had to take the risk that his theory had presented him with.

He almost phoned Marcia, but then decided against it, not wanting to increase her anxiety, to deliberately seek the comfort of someone who had once been a stranger to him but now was the most important person in his life – a woman who could assuage his loneliness and guilt, a woman with whom he could start again.

So why had he taken such a risk, just at the moment when he could escape from the past, draw a line under his guilty responsibility and try to find some happiness for a change? He could have turned his back on this lousy job. He could have been a kept man, as she had suggested.

Boyd stood staring down at the young man on the plastic see-saw for a long time, watching him throw the remains of his takeaway at a waste bin – and miss.

Pulling himself together, Boyd went to the door. He knew he had to find out if the young man was waiting for him.

Boyd slammed the door and walked across the square, shivering slightly, putting his back to his potential assassin and striding away from him, waiting for something to happen.

But nothing did happen and when he looked back he could see the young man had been waiting for an older man who was laughing and joking about being late and had an arm around the shoulders of his companion, propelling him towards the pub, talking animatedly, taking the danger away.

Boyd had been wrong and he wondered if he'd been wrong all the time and there was no conspiracy and no syndicate. He turned back towards his flat, deciding to take his car and drive to an even better takeaway a couple of miles away and bring the food back, call Marcia, reassure her and then maybe Lennox, or even Hathaway. He had to keep on the boil. He had to fathom out more, rake through the situation at Aston again. He couldn't lose momentum.

As Boyd drove away, his head ringing with argument and counter-argument, he felt increasingly nervous. The streets still seemed alive with hostility and every time he stopped at a traffic light or paused at a T-junction he looked back.

As he neared the takeaway, he felt sure he was being followed. Hadn't that red Toyota been around for too long? Then the vehicle overtook him and Boyd realised that once again he was simply being paranoid.

Reaching the takeaway, he parked the car and went inside. Having given his order, Boyd watched the small TV screen on a shelf above him, waiting for the news round-up to take in the press conference at Aston. There was a close-up of Neil Hathaway making his resignation statement and then Angela Mason reading her own longer speech. But there was no sign of Brand or, thankfully, himself. Damage limitation, he thought.

Then there was a tracking shot of Aston's bleak buildings with a voice-over. 'Three killings on the same unit in eleven days is something of a record for the British Prison Service. No one seems to know, and that includes the CID, what went wrong and whether the murders were carried out by an inmate or a prison officer or a combination of both. And now, in the wake of Governor Hathaway's resignation, Detective Inspector Lennox of the CID in the Metropolitan Division had this to say.'

Lennox came on screen, looking hunted. 'At the moment we have dozens of prison officers – and some inmates – being reinterviewed. We are hoping to make an arrest – or even a series of arrests – within the next twenty-four hours, but at the moment I can't comment any further on the motives behind the serial killings, the suspects or how the murders occurred in a maximum security unit.'

Then the reporter came on screen. 'So the police are talking about a possible conspiracy concerning the killings that have shaken the nation. A Wing, the secure

131

unit at Aston, is now shut and the remaining two prisoners are awaiting transfer to other institutions. This is Tim Harrington. *News at Ten*. Outside Aston Prison.'

Boyd picked up his takeaway order and fumbled in his pocket for his mobile. Then he realised he'd left it in the flat and swore. A few minutes later he found a telephone box and called Creighton.

'What the hell were you doing at that press conference?'

'Drawing fire.'

'That was very dangerous.'

'Time's running out. I don't choose to self-destruct, but I had to do something to make things happen. This conspiracy's been going a long time. They're buried deep and I needed to flush them out.'

'With yourself as a target?'

'I couldn't see any other alternative.' Boyd paused. 'I've got someone in my life at last. So I can assure you I don't want to take personal risks, but I knew there was no other way out.'

'I can see how the situation arose – and I'm sorry,' said Creighton. 'You're one of the best insiders we've got.'

'There really was no other way of pushing for a solution on this one,' Boyd assured him. 'And I've just seen the ITV news, but I'm not on camera.'

'But you are, albeit fleetingly, on the BBC.'

'I've been to see Hathaway.'

'And?'

'He reckons my theory is a possibility and Aston could have been set up with insiders over a long period of time.'

'The prison itself – or the unit?'

'The unit's only been in existence for a year, so probably Aston itself. I reckon it's a big operation, which isn't nearly over yet.'

'*What*?' Creighton sounded seriously alarmed again and Boyd felt a malicious pleasure. 'What do you mean, it's not over?'

'I think the killings, the closure of the unit and

Hathaway's resignation are only a beginning. There's the possibility of members of the Maxton Syndicate being sprung as well.'

'Who's behind this? Who would have the muscle and the money?'

'The law and order lobby have powerful backers. Or it could be the Maxton mafiosi.'

Boyd suddenly froze, staring through the murky glass of the phone box. For a moment he couldn't think what he was afraid of. Then he realised he'd just seen a red Toyota pass by. Sweat broke out on his forehead and Boyd tried to pull himself together. What was so unusual about seeing another red Toyota?

'What's happening?' Creighton sounded anxious.

'I've got nothing else to report.'

'What are you going to do next?'

'I'm working in the main prison at the moment. I could get access to the Maxton brothers.'

'I'd rather you were back on A Wing – closed or not. Surely it'll take a bit of time to transfer those last two inmates.'

'I don't know. But the only way of getting reinstated is to come clean to the new governor. What do you think about that?'

'Not a lot. Ever since you started this job you've been running too many risks. This is another.'

'I still think you're forgetting the deadline.' Boyd was on the defensive.

Then he saw the red Toyota pass again, this time more slowly and on his side of the street.

'You need to be careful, Danny,' Creighton was saying.

'So I've been told.'

'If the Maxton Syndicate's involved in this, you really could get taken out.'

'Don't lose sight of the fact that there might be some other basis for the killings. There could be no insiders involved. There could be no Maxton interest. It's all theory and I need hard evidence.'

133

Creighton digested the information. 'Then how the hell were the killings carried out? That number, in a secure unit? A *very* secure unit. Infiltrators *are* the only answer – and there's going to be one hell of a row at the Home Office about security.'

'That's why I'm taking the risks.'

The red Toyota had come to a halt beside the phone box. Passing motorists' headlights and the glare from a shop window were so bright that Boyd couldn't get a glimpse of the driver who was a shapeless huddle behind the wheel.

'I'd better go,' said Boyd.

'I hope you've told me everything –'

Boyd suddenly realised that he hadn't. 'If we are to support the conspiracy theory, there would have to have been a co-ordinator and Hathaway agreed that the senior prison officer on A Wing could be playing that role.'

'His name?'

'Ted Brand.'

Boyd studied the Toyota again through the glass of the telephone box. There didn't seem to be a passenger, but a light rain was beginning to fall, glistening on the road, increasing the glare, and it was still impossible to see clearly.

'Hathaway thinks there's an outside chance that Angela Mason could be involved.'

'The new governor? Don't make me laugh.'

'I'm not trying to.'

Boyd was still, gazing transfixed at the electric window of the red Toyota which was winding down, a thin barrel slowly appearing. Then the passenger, who must have been crouching down in his seat, sat up to take aim. For a moment Boyd was incredulous, unable to believe what was happening. They had finally arrived.

'Christ!' he whispered.

'What is it?'

'I was right after all. They're here.'

Boyd dropped the phone, put his shoulder to the door

and flung himself out on to the wet pavement, scattering his takeaway, rolling over until he was lying behind the telephone box and away from the road.

He could hear the bullets from the silenced gun smashing the glass as he got to his knees and then scrambled to his feet, running back the way he had come, seeking the sanctuary of the takeaway.

Glancing behind him he saw the red Toyota backing up, tyres screaming on the wet road as more bullets hit the front of Lloyds Bank. Then a woman spun round and fell to the pavement.

Boyd knew he had no time to check her out. Pushing open the door of the takeaway he knocked down a young boy and vaulted over the counter.

'We don't have any money on the premises,' the Chinese man behind the counter yelled at him.

'No one wants your money. I'm police. Stand back.'

'I can't allow you this side of the counter.' He was stubbornly persistent.

'Sorry about that.' Boyd hit him hard in the stomach and he went down.

Hearing a car door slam, he ran towards the kitchen, pushing aside the chef, looking round for the exit and grabbing the handle of a door – which was locked.

'Get me out!'

The chef didn't seem to understand what he was saying.

'Open the fucking door!' Boyd yelled.

He rattled the handle again and then put his shoulder to it, splintering the woodwork.

But still the door wouldn't budge.

Boyd threw himself at it again and this time the door gave, precipitating him into an alley that led back to the road. Someone was walking towards him with a stick. Then Boyd realised that he wasn't carrying a stick. It was a gun and he was taking aim. Boyd ducked, dived back into the kitchen again and raced towards the counter. The shop was full and Boyd couldn't work out

135

whether the crowd had come in for takeaways or to indulge in some spectator sport.

With a howl of fear and rage, Boyd threw himself at the crowd, cutting a path through the bodies. No one tried to stop him, but at one stage he fell and someone stepped on his hand.

Boyd kicked out, freed himself and got to his feet, struggling and pushing his way through to the door of the takeaway and out on to the pavement where the rain had become a downpour.

The red Toyota was parked by the kerb with its passenger door open, but the driver was still behind the wheel.

Boyd ran for his own car, fumbling for the keys, unable to find them as he ripped at his pockets.

Glancing back he saw more people gathering on the pavement, but there was no sign of pursuit. Then, to his relief, Boyd located the keys in the back pocket of his trousers, reached his car, unlocked the door and jumped inside, fumbling desperately to get started.

The engine fired at once and he backed out into the main road, turning round and skidding slightly on the wet surface, wipers racing. Glancing back he saw the red Toyota was still parked outside the takeaway but someone was now clambering into the passenger seat.

Boyd accelerated, knowing he had to lose them fast. He saw a side street coming up and twisted the wheel, tyres screaming as he turned, gunning the engine until he came to a T-junction.

Looking into the rear mirror, Boyd could see no sign of the red Toyota. Accelerating again he turned left, passing a row of parked cars and then on to a dual carriageway, all too fearful of impending pursuit, staring into his rear-view mirror until he almost veered off on to the hard shoulder and hit a parked minibus. Swerving to avoid the vehicle, noticing the interior of his car was beginning to mist up, he blasted the windscreen with hot air and accelerated again, speeding along, knowing that there was no point in going back to the flat where he was sure they would find him. Instead, he would go to Marcia's.

Be careful, said Creighton's voice in Boyd's head. *Be careful*. Surely they wouldn't find him at Marcia's? He'd shaken them off, hadn't he? Glancing into his rear mirror again he still saw no sign of pursuit. Nevertheless, Boyd continued to drive at high speed until he suddenly began to shake all over and had to slow down, his hands trembling on the wheel. After a while the shaking stopped, but an incredible thirst had seized him and he almost stopped at a service area to buy a bottle of cold water.

Be careful, came Creighton's voice again, just in time. *Be careful*.

Picking up speed again, Boyd drove on until he came to a roundabout and the dual carriageway turned into a network of urban roads. Every time he had to slow down for traffic lights, he stared into his rear mirror, waiting for the red Toyota to appear. But there was no sign of the car, and gradually he was able to convince himself that he must have lost them.

The shaking of his whole body continued as the shock of his survival began to set in. It was a miracle. He had reacted instinctively, but had never been so close to death before.

Eventually, he arrived at Marcia's flat just off the Earls Court Road, but parked his car several streets away as a precaution. Suppose she was out? What the hell would he do then? A wave of despair filled him; he felt as if he was up against such incredible odds that anything he did would be useless. Conspiracies? Infiltration? It was as if the world had turned against him. Then, slowly, Boyd began to have an unexpected feeling of triumph. He had flushed them out, had proved the conspiracy existed. They were after him, but he'd lost them.

Gasping, wiping away the sweat, Boyd sat in the Renault, watching the parked cars around him, trying to work out whether he was being watched in turn. He must have sat there for over ten minutes before feeling safe enough to get out and lock up the car.

For a few more moments he leant against the Renault, waiting and listening and staring about him. Then, impatient with himself, Boyd began to walk, his steps sounding loud on the pavement, darting glances behind him all the time.

Finally he reached the quiet garden square and checking his watch found it was after midnight. He buzzed Marcia's entryphone several times before she answered anxiously.

'Who is it?'

'Danny.'

'Come up.'

Looking behind him and then around the square, Boyd saw nothing suspicious, but when the lock clicked open he hurried into the darkened foyer, beginning to shake again. By the time he had reached Marcia's flat he was in a state of raw panic.

'What's happened?' She was standing in a dressing gown, looking uneasy.

'I need shelter.'

'You've found it.'

'Thanks.' He shut and locked the door, leaning against it.

'What's happened?'

'I'll tell you in a moment.'

'Can I get you something?'

'Just some cold water.'

He followed Marcia into the kitchen, listening to the reassuring hum of the fridge and watching her take out a bottle and pour the cold water into a glass. He grabbed at it, drained the water and asked for more.

Then the entryphone buzzed again.

'Christ!'

'What's the matter?'

'I was certain I wasn't being followed. But now I'm not so sure.'

'What shall I do?'

Boyd thought furiously. Then he made a decision. 'Find out who it is.'

Marcia went to the intercom. 'Who's there?'

There was a slight pause and then a voice said, 'Police.'

'What do you want?'

'Can I speak to Mr Taylor?'

Marcia gazed at Boyd in confusion, not knowing what to do.

He hesitated. Then he went over to the intercom and snapped, 'Taylor.'

'Mr Luke Taylor?'

'Yes.'

'Police.'

'Identify yourself.'

'PC Raymond Wynn.'

'Number?'

'195632.'

'What do you want?'

'Just making sure you're safe, sir.'

'How did you know I was here?'

'We've been checking.'

'What do you mean – checking?'

'I gather you had a bit of bother in a Chinese take-away.'

'You could say that.'

'When your conversation in the telephone box on Hastings Street was interrupted, a squad car was sent to investigate. A passer-by was shot in the leg and is being treated in hospital. A tail was put on you, but now we know you're here and safe, we'll leave you to recover. You've obviously suffered a very unpleasant experience.'

'OK.' Boyd relaxed a little. 'Thanks for coming out.'

'That's all right, sir. Try and get some rest.'

'Goodnight.' Boyd gazed blankly at Marcia who gave him another glass of cold water. He gulped the liquid down, slaking his thirst and feeling a little calmer. But he still couldn't work out whether the police officer was for real or not.

His panic returned for now his whereabouts had been clearly established. Fine if they were the police, but if they weren't . . .

'We can't stay here,' he said.

'Why not?'

'I have a gunman after me.'

'Christ!'

'I shouldn't have come here. We need to get out and back into the car.'

'But the police just called.'

'I don't know if they *are* the police.'

'Look – I've got good security here. The entryphone. The locks. Won't we be safer here?'

Boyd's thoughts raced as fatigue swept him. 'All right.' But as he spoke he knew he was taking another appalling risk. 'I suppose it's possible that I was looking so hard for a red Toyota that I missed a squad car,' he said slowly, trying to convince himself.

'Do you want to go to bed?'

'With you?'

'Or alone if you're stressed out.'

'I'm absolutely stressed out, but I still want to go to bed with you.'

Marcia took Boyd in her arms and kissed him. 'Do you want to talk about it?'

'No.'

'What are you going to do tomorrow?'

'I have to go back to work.'

'Are you nearly finished?'

'I hope so. And I've made a decision. I'm going back into the Met as a DI.'

'I wish you'd leave the police altogether.'

'How can I?'

'I've got some money – an income from my father's shares.'

Boyd looked uneasy.

'Could you live with that?' she asked suspiciously.

'Maybe. You're tempting me.'

'That's what I want to do.'

'Look – I'll have to make just one call. Have you got a mobile?'

He rang Creighton and Marcia went into the sitting room.

'What happened?'

'I was right.'

'There's a civilian casualty.'

'Did you send a squad car after me?'

'Yes.'

'Thank God. You don't know the officer's name?'

'No. Suppose I could find out.'

'I'd be grateful if you did. He gave me PC Raymond Wynn. Number 195632.'

'What happened?' Creighton repeated.

'They tried to kill me.'

'Where are you?'

'In a friend's flat in London.'

'Stay where you are.'

'I've got to go into Aston tomorrow.'

'I wouldn't advise that.'

'I've got to. I was right about the conspiracy. I must have been.'

'You've still got no real proof.'

'What about tonight?' Boyd interrupted, his temper rising.

Creighton was silent. Then he said. 'You need protection.'

'Insiders don't get protection.'

'Are you armed?'

'No. The gun's in the flat.'

'What about Mason? Are you going to confide in her?'

'I've decided that's too risky.'

'To have gone out unarmed was an appalling risk. I'll organise more back-up.'

'Thanks.'

'Give me your number. I'll call you back.'

As he hung up, Marcia came back into the room with a couple of glasses.

'Let's have a drink – soft of course – before we go to bed.'

Boyd followed her back into the sitting room and they sat down on the sofa.

'Are you in trouble?'

'Yes. But the police are giving me back-up.'

'What does that mean?'

'Plain-clothes officers sitting in a car, making sure no one gets in here without authorisation.' Boyd leant back and closed his eyes. Then suddenly he sat up again. 'Is there a caretaker here?'

'Yes.'

Boyd got up and went to the window. Pulling aside the curtain a little he could see cars were densely parked on the resident-permit meters. Any of them could be playing a waiting game.

Boyd lay beside Marcia after they had had sex, more relaxed yet still apprehensive, wondering when Creighton would ring.

'That was good,' she said.

'Adrenalin,' he muttered.

Sleep was slowly overtaking them and as they lay in each other's arms the silence about them seemed deep, comforting and secure. Boyd's eyes closed and slowly the reality of the happiness he had found with Marcia became absolute – a certainty that was like some miraculous bastion.

For over two years he had hidden in other identities, other people's worlds, trying to ward off his grief and the guilt that went with it. But now, for the first time, he was Daniel Boyd again. And Daniel had a future.

As he slipped deeper into sleep, the trauma of what had happened in the takeaway began to recede. He began to make hazy plans and saw himself and Marcia walking on the South Downs on a breezy spring day, beginning to run downhill towards the sea. They were holding hands and –

'I think there's someone in the flat,' Marcia whispered.

'I can't hear anything.' Boyd sat up and listened. 'No one could have got in. We've got protection.'

But Creighton hadn't rung and when Boyd glanced at his watch he saw that an hour had passed. What the hell was Creighton doing? He should have rung by now.

'I thought I heard the kitchen door to the fire escape open – as if it had been quietly forced. But maybe I'm overreacting.'

Boyd froze. He had heard a small sound, but wasn't sure what it was. He got out of bed, naked, listening intently.

'Maybe I was mistaken,' Marcia whispered.

'Yes.' But Boyd was still straining his ears for the slightest sound. Still he could hear nothing. 'I think you were mistaken,' he muttered.

Boyd walked over to the phone and dialled Creighton's number.

'Yes?'

'Why didn't you ring?'

'Because they're trying to trace your police officer.'

'You mean he doesn't exist?'

'I'll try them again.'

'Look, what about the protection?'

'They're on their way. Should be with you any minute.'

'You should have called.'

'I'm sorry.'

'It's important to trace this police officer.'

'OK. I'll let you know as soon as I can.'

Boyd put the phone down gently – and heard what he thought was a light footstep. He put a finger to his lips, his mind reeling, wondering what to do, glancing across at Marcia, who was still sitting up in bed, clasping the duvet. Her lips moved but no sound came.

143

Boyd went through to the sitting room and picked up a heavy frosted glass vase from a little table.

'That's an antique,' she hissed involuntarily, standing naked in the doorway.

'It's a weapon,' Boyd whispered.

There was no sound now and he had the feeling that someone was standing behind the kitchen door, just like he was, poised and anxious, waiting to see what would happen.

I've got to move fast, thought Boyd. I've got to take the initiative.

He grasped the door knob, which rattled slightly. Now he had lost the advantage. Now he had given himself away.

Still nothing happened, but he was sure he could feel a presence. Someone *had* to be there, waiting while he was waiting. But that someone could be armed.

Boyd signalled to Marcia to move back into the bedroom, but she shook her head, looking away from him, staring at the kitchen door. Then Boyd heard what he was sure was a sharp intake of breath.

He had to take the initiative.

And that's what the intruder's thinking, thought Boyd. If there's anyone there at all. Waiting, naked and with a frosted glass vase in his hand, he suddenly felt ridiculous. There had to be an explanation. He glanced at his watch. It was just after 2 a.m. What about his back-up? A flood of relief filled him. Of course. That was it. His protection had arrived, and here they were, both stark naked. Boyd almost laughed aloud. But in the back of his mind he knew his relief was false. Why *should* his protection break in?

'What the hell are you doing?' Marcia had caught his mood of indecision.

'It must be one of our people,' he said determinedly. 'We're going to be OK. Go and get into a dressing gown and let me have something to wear. What have you got?'

'I've got a couple of dressing gowns,' she admitted.

144

'For the men in your life?' Boyd tried to joke and failed badly.

When she brought back the dressing gown, Boyd put it on quickly.

'Sorry about all that,' he said. 'I'd better go and reassure them we're still in one piece.'

'Don't do that,' she whispered.

'Why not?'

'Because you're not sure.'

Boyd hesitated, but he'd had enough waiting. More than enough.

He flung the door open.

Boyd was certain he was gazing into the eyes of the same man he had seen in the alley and who had pursued him back into the takeaway.

He felt a sense of being badly let down and then the old, more familiar guilt. He'd bogged it all up.

'Get back in the bedroom!' he shouted at Marcia.

He hit out with the vase and caught the intruder on the shoulder. Taking care not to lose his grip on the vase, he hit him again, this time catching him in the face.

In the back of his mind he was wondering if he had really heard the dull thud of a silenced automatic. And where had that gasp come from?

Oblivious to the danger he was in, Boyd swung round to see Marcia clasping her chest where the blood was welling up in a great gout.

'Oh, Christ!' he yelled and turned back, hitting out again and again, finding himself soaked with blood that wasn't his own and watching the intruder toppling backwards with a little grunt of pain. Then Boyd ran back to Marcia who was choking, sounding as if she was drowning, with the red blood still welling out of her chest.

Another bullet thudded into the wall and then a mirror cracked in the darkness. Boyd had thought he had knocked his assailant unconscious, or even that he'd

145

killed him, but he turned to see the man kneeling, bleeding from the head, but clasping the automatic with both hands. There was blood in his eyes and a cut on his forehead that seemed to expose some bone.

Again and again, Boyd drove the vase into his face. Eventually the glass shattered into a mass of fragments and this time the intruder lay still, a foot jerking, his eyes widening, and then he was still.

Staggering away, Boyd switched on the light and ran back to Marcia whose eyes were glazing, the blood continuing to pump out of her chest.

He grabbed the duvet cover and ripped at it, tearing out a section and trying to plug the hole. But still the blood poured through. Would it never stop?

He ran to the phone, dialled 999 and got through, yelling out the words POLICE and AMBULANCE and giving the address. As he did so, he could hear the entryphone buzzing.

Boyd grabbed the gun from the man on the floor whose wide-open eyes were gazing up at him with a kind of puzzled concern. As he answered the entryphone, he realised their assailant was dead.

'Police,' said the voice, and when he let them in there were three of them, all clutching ID cards, running towards Marcia, the blood still spurting through her clasped hands.

'She's in big trouble,' yelled one of the plain-clothes officers. 'Have you called an ambulance?'

'Yes,' said Boyd, standing by the door, gazing at Marcia who was still pumping blood. 'So much for protection,' he shouted. 'Who is this guy? Who the fuck is he?'

The dead man lay on his back, young with dark hair and a moustache, small, almost puny. His automatic now lay on the sofa, where Boyd had dropped it.

'God knows,' said the police officer. 'I'm DC Laughton. Stay here. There may be more of them.'

Producing handguns, they checked through the flat, backing each other up as they crept into each room.

When they'd finished and found no one, Boyd shouted, 'Can you do something for her?' He sat next to Marcia on the bed, tearing up more of the duvet cover in a desperate attempt to staunch the gaping hole in her chest.

'Leave her to the paramedics,' said Laughton, hovering in the doorway while his two colleagues spoke urgently into their mobiles.

'She'll be dead before they get here –' Boyd broke off as to his intense relief he heard the sound of a siren.

As he waited, Boyd deeply regretted drawing their fire. He had never thought for a moment that Marcia would be their victim – and not him. Not him at all.

'You're going to be all right,' he said to her, over and over again, still unsuccessfully trying to staunch the blood while the bed turned red about him. 'You're going to be all right.' She muttered something and Boyd yelled at her. 'Don't give up. For Christ's sake – don't give up now!'

'What happened?' she gasped.

'He shot you.'

'Who?'

'It doesn't matter.'

Marcia began to make the choking sound again and then spluttered, 'I love you.' Suddenly the blood began to run out of her mouth, streaming down her neck towards the hole in her chest which was still pumping out a constant red flow. 'How bad am I?' Marcia whispered.

'You'll be OK. The ambulance is here.'

Laughton opened the door to the paramedics who ran towards Marcia, pulling open their bags and extracting bandages and lint and cotton wool. This time the hole in her chest was being plugged more effectively. Then the paramedics raced back to the door and returned with a stretcher on which they gently positioned her.

'I'll come with you,' said Boyd.

'No.' Laughton seemed to be aiming his weapon at Boyd's head.

'I've got to go with her.'

'Move and I'll shoot,' shouted Laughton, and for a terrible moment Boyd, utterly confused and in shock, imagined he'd been duped yet again.

Meanwhile the paramedics were taking the stretcher awkwardly out of the open door and Boyd tried to push past Laughton while the other two plain-clothes officers stood back.

Then Laughton hit Boyd hard around the side of the head and the blackness came.

Boyd staggered to his feet and sat down on the blood-soaked bed and wept.

'I'm sorry,' said Laughton. 'You've got to stay with us. They could be waiting anywhere outside. We must talk. The medics will look after her.'

Eventually Boyd managed to tell Laughton what had happened and a few moments later Creighton phoned and Boyd explained all over again, conscious that Marcia could already be dead – and her death, like his family's, would be his responsibility.

'I was sure I wasn't followed here,' he told Creighton.

'Drawing their fire was a huge risk. I'm desperately sorry about your friend. We'll have every prison officer questioned yet again.'

'She's dying,' said Boyd bleakly, the bruise on his head beginning to throb badly.

'I suggest you stay where you are for the night while Forensic deals with everything. Then we'll have to get you back into Aston.'

'To hell with Aston! What about Marcia?'

'Your friend's getting the best possible treatment. Call the hospital and keep in touch, but don't go there. Whatever you do.'

When Creighton had rung off, Boyd called the hospital and eventually got through to Casualty, giving Marcia's name.

'Are you a relative?' a nurse asked.

'I'm a friend. She was shot while she was with me. I need to know how she is.'

The nurse went to ask and returned quickly for which Boyd was deeply grateful.

'She's being taken to the operating theatre. We're doing all we can for her.'

'Is she going to die?'

'I can't give you any more information. She'll be in theatre soon. They're doing their best for her.'

'What kind of state was she in on admission?'

'Very poorly. I'm afraid I really can't tell you any more.'

'You've been very helpful.' Boyd tried hard to keep control and just succeeded. 'Thank you.'

When he put the phone down, Boyd sat on the blood-soaked bed while the plain-clothes officers tactfully left him alone. Precious. The word blazed across his mind. Marcia was precious. And like his family she'd been taken away.

Laughton came up to him and stood there awkwardly, obviously trying to avoid a stream of clichés, but finding nothing to say. Eventually he put his hand on Boyd's shoulder and said, 'They'll be doing their best for her.'

'So they say.'

'We'll stay here tonight and then I'll drive you to Aston in the morning. We need to try and normalise the situation as much as we can. I'm sorry I had to hit you. Do you want someone to look at that?'

'No.'

'You have to keep going now we know you're right.'

'I should never have come here. I completely under-estimated their surveillance. As far as I can tell, I've underestimated everything about them.'

'Some of these cartels are very sophisticated.'

'Would you call them a cartel?'

'The Maxtons smuggle drugs into the country on a very large scale.'

'Where from?'

'Asia and South America.'

'You know about the Maxtons?'

'Yes,' said Laughton. 'They've got all the clout of a multinational. I think Creighton felt that the less you knew –'

'The more I'd cock it up. Marcia and I were planning –' Boyd broke off. 'Look – I lost my family. That's why I came into this shit. Now I've lost my friend. If only to God I hadn't come back here.'

Laughton said nothing, and Boyd knew there was nothing he *could* say. He'd made a mistake. That was all. Another mistake – the mistake of his lifetime. He wouldn't get another chance of happiness.

'My cover's blown,' said Boyd.

'Not with the prison officers.'

'So I'm to be taken back to Aston. Isn't that – too risky for everyone?'

'I don't know. I'm protecting you,' snapped Laughton, 'not sharing your caseload.'

Boyd got up from the bed and went into the kitchen. Then he restlessly returned, believing he had to keep moving, keep walking to and fro. He had nowhere to go.

'What now?'

'We wait for Forensic.'

'Suppose this place is being watched? That guy wouldn't have come on his own. So where's the getaway car?'

'We didn't see one.'

'That doesn't mean it wasn't there.'

'I'll need to take a statement from you about the takeaway episode, as well as what happened here.'

'I was so sure I wasn't being followed.'

'Maybe you weren't,' said Laughton. 'Maybe they'd already got this address.'

'How?'

'You could have been under surveillance for a long time.'

'So my cover was blown early on? You mean I didn't need to draw their fire at all?' Boyd was incredulous.

'Not necessarily, but we just don't know.'

Eventually Boyd went to the sitting room and sat on a hard chair, glad to be talking, not wanting to stop, as if he was back-tracking in time, going to a point where he hadn't brought them to her.

Half-way through he rang the hospital, only to be told that Marcia was still in the operating theatre.

Eventually, Forensic arrived and the statement taking was again interrupted as Boyd returned to the phone, hoping to get the ever-patient nurse yet again.

'Are you the gentleman who keeps phoning about Marcia Williams?' The voice was different and more authoritative.

'Yes.'

'I think it would be better if we rang you. Now what –'

'Is she still in the operating theatre?'

'Yes.'

'How much longer is she going to be in there?'

'I've no idea, but if I can take your –'

'Is she going to die?'

'She's very poorly.'

'What does that mean?'

'I'm sorry, Mr Taylor. I'll ring you back if you give me your number.'

Chapter Eleven

Earls Court, London
23 June 2001 – 0500 hours

Boyd spent a sleepless night, sure that Marcia had died, phoning the hospital at least another half-dozen times, only to be told that she was 'poorly'. With half her chest blown away, he had no doubt that the ridiculous word was all too true, and his remorse grew as the night wore on. In the end he sat in the kitchen, completing his statement and using Laughton as a sounding board, railing at his own stupidity in even attempting to find sanctuary with Marcia.

'I might as well have been her executioner,' he said for what seemed like the hundredth time as Laughton brewed more coffee while his two colleagues assisted the forensic team in the other room.

Eventually Lennox arrived and promptly took over from Laughton.

'You can't blame yourself like this,' said Lennox. 'You came here in good faith.'

'I should never have been such a damn fool to underestimate their surveillance capabilities.'

Lennox sighed and said, 'You've done what you set out to do – make them show their hand. You've established the existence of a substantial conspiracy at Aston, and we're immensely grateful to you. I'm only sorry our protection wasn't in place quicker.'

'But if only I hadn't come here –'

'I'm very sorry about what's happened,' Lennox repeated.

'How do you think I feel?'

'I can only say again that we had no idea of the kind of organisation we were up against. Now we do. You've proved you were right. This is a tremendous coup and you've given us a huge advantage. We know what we're dealing with now.'

'Have you made arrests?'

'Not yet, but –'

'So all I've achieved is proof of a conspiracy, and I've done it at considerable human cost. By not thinking through what I was trying to achieve, I panicked and led them here – led the bastards to someone I deeply love and value. For Christ's sake – he shot her in the chest.'

'They're –'

'Doing their best for her. Don't give me that shit. I have to get down to that fucking hospital.'

'You can't. You still have work to do.'

'Why should I care?'

'You've pulled off a coup. Now you've got to get back into Aston and finish the job.'

'My cover's blown.'

'Not entirely. You still have a chance of handling the situation. We can protect you – up to a point.'

'Thanks.'

'But there's a job to finish – and it's down to you.'

'I've got to talk to Mason and Farley,' Boyd agreed. 'But how can I keep in touch with the hospital? Can you lend me a mobile?'

Lennox nodded. 'Find out who's behind all this.'

'And then?'

'We'll wrap it up,' said Lennox.

Wearying of the conversation, exhausted and drained, Boyd dragged the sitting-room sofa into the spacious kitchen and slept, oblivious to the forensic team still at work in the sitting room and bedroom and the plain-clothes police officers making coffee.

He dreamed of Marcia with the hole in her chest pumping blood over the bed while he did his hopelessly inadequate best to stem the flow. The stream became wider and more fast-flowing until he was overtaken by a great tidal wave of blood on which his dead family, Abbie, Rick and Mary, were hurtling along on a raft.

He woke to a dry mouth, the knowledge that an unidentifiable tragedy had occurred and DI Laughton bringing him a mug of black coffee.

'Where's Lennox?' he croaked.

'Gone.'

'Forensic?'

'They've packed up and gone too. We're here to see you get safely into Aston this morning.'

Then the realisation came and Boyd staggered to his feet and dialled the hospital number, eventually getting a nurse he had spoken to before.

'Miss Williams is still in recovery.'

Boyd looked down at his watch and saw that only a couple of hours had passed while he had had his nightmare-laden sleep.

'Can't you tell me anything?'

'I'm really sorry I can't tell you any more. Ring us a little later.'

Boyd put the phone down and turned to Laughton. 'Get me to Aston.'

'You should eat something.' Laughton produced a plate of burnt toast. 'I can't find any marmalade.'

'Fuck the marmalade,' said Boyd.

He knew he had to find the mental reserves to return to Aston, work through his shift and try to contact Mason and Farley.

Boyd was driven in an unmarked police car to a side street a few hundred metres from the gates of Aston and he walked the rest of the way, tailed by two plain-clothes officers, checking every car. He dreaded the return of the red Toyota, although he knew they would never use the vehicle again. But, to Boyd, the Toyota was a symbol of death.

He tried to be rational. The Maxton cartel – as Laughton had called them – would have traced not only his own address, but Marcia's as well. His telephone calls would have been intercepted and his credentials checked, not necessarily because he was suspected of being an undercover police officer, but because he was a new face and the fact that he had not worked for the prison service before would have been noted.

Boyd blamed his lack of grip. Marcia had received a horrendous injury. Perhaps she was already dead.

Suppose Angela Mason *was* part of the infiltration team? It was possible. Then Boyd began to swing the other way and was soon sure that her involvement was highly unlikely. Mason was too high up, too inaccessible to the infiltrators. She wouldn't be able to control them as effectively as someone in middle management and close to the grass roots. Someone like Brand, or even Farley. Someone who knew him even if he didn't yet know them. But by now Boyd had convinced himself that Marcia was going to die so nothing that might happen to him seemed to matter. His glimpse of a new life had been blown out like a candle in a few seconds.

He turned the corner and Aston lay before him, the Victorian Gothic buildings only half visible behind the wall.

He tried the hospital again, but the line was busy.

Somehow Boyd got through the morning, checking the prisoners and monitoring a new inmate who was thought to be suicidal.

The prisoner simply sat on his bed with his hands over his eyes, deeply depressed and immobile. During Boyd's stint of duty, the prison doctor came to see him, inducing some reluctant movement as the new inmate took off his shirt and was checked over. But once the

examination was over, he returned to his almost cata-
tonic state.

As Boyd let the doctor out, he said, 'Clinical depres-
sion. I'll prescribe him something.'

Boyd found the doctor's examination cursory, lacking
interest or compassion. He was simply a dull cipher in
a daily grind.

When Boyd was relieved by Ray Digby, a prison
officer he hadn't met before, he told him about the
doctor's diagnosis.

'He'll have told the boss,' said Digby. 'We don't have
to do anything.' He paused and then added. 'I see we're
still in the headlines.'

Boyd nodded, unable to react to anything other than
Marcia's plight. He knew he wasn't allowed to use a
mobile while on duty and didn't want to draw attention
to himself by breaking the rules.

'I suppose it'll blow over.'

'Maybe,' said Boyd, trying to show interest. 'But serial
killing in a high security unit without an arrest seems to
be the sort of news that might just hang around.'

'At least we'll get ourselves a new governor.'

'Didn't you like Hathaway?' Boyd was desperate to
get away, but once again didn't want to draw attention
to himself.

'The guy was too liberal for me. That lifers' wing was
a huge mistake. I gather it was run like a luxury
hotel.'

Boyd didn't have the energy to put Digby right. 'How
would you like to see them treated?'

'Lock the bastards up. It's meant to be a life sentence
– not a cushy number. That's what the public want and
that's what I want.'

'What about the death sentence?'

'That would solve everything. Even locking up seems
too good for some of them.'

The officer was young, with a baby face and fair hair.
Boyd would have liked to hit him hard.

He was just about to leave when the prisoner suddenly got up and began to hurl himself against the walls of his cell, bawling obscenities.

Digby drew his baton and looked at Boyd, clearly expecting him to do the same. Reluctantly, Boyd decided he had to take the initiative and do what was expected of him.

'Shut your mouth!' he yelled above the obscenities. 'If you don't, you'll get hurt.'

'Really hurt,' Digby added maliciously.

The inmate stopped shouting and returned to sitting on his bed, head in hands, and there was silence again.

Boyd glanced down at his watch which read 11.15. 'I'm going for my break,' he said. 'See you later.'

Digby nodded, gazing at the prisoner, willing him to break his silence again.

Boyd phoned the hospital from what he hoped was a quiet corridor and this time got a response. When he had given Marcia's name, the nurse said, 'Are you a relative?'

'I'm her fiancé.'

'I see. Well −'

'Please tell me,' said Boyd. 'Is she alive or dead?'

The nurse said, 'Are we talking about Marcia Williams?'

'For God's sake. You've got to tell me −'

'She's very ill.'

Well, at least she hadn't used the dread word 'poorly'. 'What about the operation?'

'She's in intensive care.'

A tiny spark of hope suddenly ignited. 'Can't you tell me whether she's going to live?'

'She's comfortable.'

'Is she going to live?' shouted Boyd, the strain unbearable, and a group of prison officers hurrying towards the canteen turned to stare at him over their shoulders.

'I just can't tell you.' The nurse was trying to be

humane, and in the back of his mind Boyd knew that, but he was breaking up, barely able to cope, sweat pouring off him.

'Tell me something. Is she conscious?'

'She slips in and out.'

'What do you think? What are her chances?' Boyd was pleading now.

'I really can't tell you that.'

'Can I come in and see her this evening?'

'You say you're her fiancé? Come when you can.'

'Will you tell her something from me?' He lowered his voice. 'Tell her it's Danny calling. Tell Marcia I love her.'

'I'll make sure your message gets through.'

'Thank you.' Boyd put the mobile back in his pocket and with tears in his eyes went into the canteen, hoping to find Bill Farley.

He saw him sitting at a table in the corner. When he saw Boyd, he gave him a wary smile.

'I'm sorry,' he said as Boyd sat down. 'You seem to have some personal trouble.'

Boyd stared at him.

'I passed you in the corridor when you were talking on your mobile. Forgive me if I'm speaking out of turn.'

'Friend of mine's sick. She's got cancer,' he added.

'What are the chances?'

'Fifty fifty.'

'I'm sorry,' he said again. 'You seem to be in the wars.'

The cliché was more comforting than irritating.

'You may have noticed I've been taken off the unit.'

'That was a great pity. Rhodes asked after you. He seemed to regard you as my trusty stand-in.'

'I'd never replace you.'

'I'm afraid I'll have to be replaced. Rhodes is going to Broadmoor.'

'When?'

'In a couple of days.'

'Is everyone going to lose their job? With the closure of the unit?'

'Afraid so. But I've decided to take early retirement.'

'What will you do?'

'I thought I'd go on a cruise.'

'That sounds good.' Boyd was floundering as he tried to show interest.

'It's something to do.' Boyd's lacklustre attitude seemed to be contagious.

'Will you miss the job?'

'No. I'm up to here with it – and the closure of the unit is the final nail in the coffin for me.' He was suddenly very angry.

'What do you think of the change of governor?'

'Appalling. Hathaway had real vision.'

'What about Angela Mason?'

'A politically correct little bureaucrat.'

'I didn't realise Ted Brand was so against A Wing.'

'How did you know that?' Farley seemed uneasy.

'He told me.'

Farley appeared to relax a little. 'Always has been.'

'So why head up A Wing?'

'He's ambitious – but he won't take risks.'

'It would be great to have a drink sometime,' said Boyd.

'Why not?' said Farley. 'We could drown our sorrows.'

He's a great man for clichés, thought Boyd, but which side is he on?

'What about tonight?'

Farley seemed to hesitate. Then he said, 'Yes. That would be fine. How about the Rising Sun?'

'Where's that?'

'Down Yardley Street. Five minutes from here.' Farley paused. 'I seem to have missed out on some high drama.'

'What do you think's going on?' asked Boyd.

'God knows. I can't make any sense out of it at all.'

'I hear you've got a daughter.' Boyd was once again acting on instinct.

'Yes. Who told you?' Farley was oddly defensive.

'Rhodes,' he lied.

'Yes. I've got a daughter. She's called Liz. Her mother walked out on us a long time ago and we divorced.'

'Is she at college or –'

'She's at Highlands – studying to be a teacher.'

'What does she specialise in?'

'Drama. She's in her last year. Somehow we rub along together.'

'Rhodes must know a lot about you.'

'He does. I know a lot about him, too.'

'Do you think he's capable of killing again?'

Farley shrugged.

'Could he be involved in these murders?'

'He was seen on the monitors every time. There's no way he could have killed them. Why are you so anxious to know all this?'

'I just wondered if he could have been used.'

'I've heard there's a conspiracy theory going the rounds, but infiltration would've had to be almost total for Rhodes to have been let out of his cell and then got back again.'

'Have you ever been afraid of him?'

'Only once.' Farley paused and then continued without being prompted. 'I'd let him down on some research matter and he lost his temper.'

'What happened?'

'He said he knew where I lived and that he was able to get out of A Wing whenever he chose and he'd do just that – and kill my daughter. He threatened to cut Liz up and throw her body parts in the Thames. He later withdrew the threat.'

'That must have been a nasty moment.'

'It was. Liz is my life. I worried about the threat for weeks.'

Boyd remembered the tiny figure in the bed – in her father's bed. She had looked more like a child than a student.

The bell began to sound and they both got up. 'See you in the boozer,' said Boyd.

'What's life like outside A Wing?' asked Farley curiously.

'Predictable.'

'Why did Brand get rid of you? I thought you were doing well.'

'Thanks.'

'So why?'

Boyd paused. 'I started to ask too many questions.'

'What's wrong with that?'

'Then I spoke up at the press conference – in favour of A Wing.'

'Good for you.' Farley paused. 'You do ask a lot of questions,' he said. 'But no doubt there's a reason for that.'

'I saw something I admired, almost fleetingly, get sabotaged. I was very impressed with A Wing. I wasn't prepared to let it go.'

Farley shrugged. 'What has to be . . .'

'Are you into the conspiracy theory?'

'I haven't had time to think. Like your friend, my daughter has a health problem.'

'Can I ask a question about that?'

'Sure. She's always been too small for her age – and she's been getting hormone treatment which has gone wrong. Liz has bouts of nausea. Severe nausea. But I can't get any answers from the medical people.'

'Your GP?'

'The consultant. He's evasive.' Farley began to move away, heading back in the direction of A Wing. 'I don't know what's happening to her.' His voice broke.

'I want to see the governor.'

'I'm afraid she's busy right now.'

The secretary had a striking similarity to the nurse at the hospital. Polite, but evasive.

'I think she'll see me if you tell her who it is. It's Taylor – Luke Taylor – from C Wing.'

'A Mr Taylor. You'll see him? Very well.' She looked at Boyd disapprovingly. 'You can go in.'

'Thank you.' Boyd walked across the beige carpet to the governor's office and knocked. Before Angela Mason could reply he had opened the door.

She was sitting in an armchair that had been turned round to face over the outside association area in which groups of inmates were milling around, some kicking a ball, others in what seemed like apathetic conversation. Over a dozen prison officers were mingling with them. What is she doing? Boyd wondered, and then had the almost surreal impression that Angela Mason was engaged in some sort of surveillance exercise. She seemed preoccupied.

'Do sit down.'

Boyd took an armchair and turned it round so that he, too, could watch the association area.

'I was expecting you.'

'Really?' Boyd tensed.

'Neil told me about you.'

Boyd felt a lurch of sudden insecurity and then anger. Why had Hathaway interfered? Why had he taken a risk that he wasn't authorised to take? Boyd then remembered that *he* had proposed taking the risk and Hathaway had tried to deter him.

'I was sorry not to have had the information earlier. Did you think I was part of this conspiracy too?'

She smiled hesitantly at him and Boyd wondered how much to tell her. 'I take it that you're now aware I'm a police officer working undercover.'

'Yes.'

'Mr Hathaway told you about it.'

'I think he was reluctant at first, and then changed his mind.'

Boyd felt completely cynical. Even Hathaway, he thought.

'Neil and I never got on. He didn't find it easy to take me into his confidence,' she explained.

'Why not?'

'I was too much the Home Secretary's golden girl – although you'd be unwise to take that too literally.'

'I need to get back on A Wing,' said Boyd abruptly.

'Isn't that too risky?'

'In what way?'

'Your reappearance would be put down to intervention from on high. And that's the last thing you need.'

'I was hoping for more subtle readmittance.'

'I don't think there is such a thing.'

Boyd felt blocked. Was she right – would his reappearance be too obvious?

'I gather you need to talk to Farley. Can't you approach him some other way?'

'I'm seeing him tonight.'

Her expression was inscrutable. 'On what basis?'

'Social.'

'Are you expecting him to help you in your investigation? Are you going to tell him who you are?'

'No. I'm still in the decent young prison officer with a conscience role.'

'You'll have to be careful with that. It's not as credible as you would like to think.'

Boyd had the distinct impression that even though Angela Mason had been told who he was, she was not going to be as co-operative as she might be. Again he wondered how much she could be trusted. Hathaway had said *he* didn't trust her, so it seemed odd that he'd told her anything at all. But the trouble with conspiracy theories was that they could be blown up like a balloon – until they burst. If Mason was in on it then why not Hathaway too? There was no stopping the ever widening scenario.

'I don't have time to be careful,' Boyd snapped. That had always been the problem. Lack of time. He'd had to think on his feet throughout this disastrous investigation.

163

'I hear you've got close to Farley in your undercover role.'

'Hardly. He's been away.'

'He doesn't suspect you?'

'I hope not, but I can't be sure. The whole operation has been botched because of short cuts.'

'But you have my ear.'

'What can you tell me?'

'I think the infiltration theory is difficult to prove.'

'In what way?'

'Because everyone is suspect. Including me. I could easily be the spider at the centre of your web.'

'Yes.'

'And just as easily not be.'

Boyd shrugged.

'Do you know if anyone suspects you?' she asked.

'Yes. They tried to kill me last night.' Boyd described the previous night's events, including the shooting of Marcia.

'I had no idea the problem was running out of control like this,' she said and Boyd could see she was shocked. 'I'm very sorry to hear about your friend,' she added, but now he thought she seemed distant, detached.

'I have police protection, but I don't think the Met – or anyone else – knew the scale of it all.'

'Did Neil accept your theory?'

'Increasingly. Didn't he tell you?'

'He didn't mention it.'

'And yet he told you about me. When was that?'

'Last night.'

'What time?'

'About eight. I think you'd just left his home.'

'You could have ordered my execution if you're part of the team.'

'I never was a good team player. Obviously I can't reassure you either way. But it should be sufficient to say that I have ambitions and they lie more in the future of the prison service – particularly in the future of this particular prison – than in the criminal underworld. I don't have too much experience of that.'

'I take it you were opposed to Hathaway's project?'

'I was initially interested in the experiment, but A Wing didn't work for me.'

'Why was that?'

'There were too many privileges. Too much laxity. There wasn't sufficient attention being paid to retraining the inmates.'

'But they were staying put. Life was for life.'

'Nevertheless, they could have been much more usefully deployed. I also thought the exclusivity of their lives was inappropriate.'

'You wanted them to be treated more severely?'

'No. But I want prisons to share responsibility for the kind of criminal with a real life sentence. They shouldn't be given special treatment, and I didn't like the idea of Aston being dumped with a whole bunch of them. That kind of inmate should be distributed around the country.'

'What about Brand?'

'He shares my views at last. It took him some time.'

'And Farley?'

'I've no idea. I don't know him well enough. Is there any other way I can be useful?' she asked abruptly, as if his time had run out.

'I don't think so.'

'I'm sorry I can't reinstate you. But I feel that would be giving too much away.'

'Maybe you're right.'

Angela Mason stood up, dismissing him. 'I've got a busy day working my way into the job,' she said. 'But if you need any more help, you know where to find me.'

'Suppose there's no conspiracy? Suppose the killings were carried out some other way?' Boyd wanted to make her uneasy.

'Surely security makes that impossible?'

'Are you sure?'

'I've thought it through carefully.' She paused. 'I'm very sorry about your friend. I hope she recovers.'

'So do I.' Boyd turned away. 'My job isn't enviable,' he said.

'No.' Angela Mason spoke slowly. 'I know it isn't – and never could be.'

As he opened the door into the outer office, Boyd felt curiously exposed. He had to be watchful, even inside Aston. There was no one to protect him here.

The day dragged past without incident, but Boyd felt increasingly oppressed, as if he had been caught in a net and was gradually being pulled on to a dark and malevolent shore. Slowly he began to see the infiltrators as a giant octopus with transparent tentacles that were hard to define but were everywhere.

He had surreptitiously phoned the hospital several times, getting different members of staff, but always the same irritating answer: poorly. He kept wondering what they would say if she had died. Would the answer be: poorly but dead?

With his shift over, conscious of having wasted valuable time, Boyd left Aston, checking himself through security to the front gates.

Glancing up and down the street he saw a young woman hurrying towards him, looking agitated.

'I thought I'd lost you,' she said.

'Sorry?'

'I'm WPC Grant. Lucy Grant. I'm here to look after you. Where are you going?'

'Can you take me to the hospital?'

'I've just come from there.'

Boyd froze. Had she been sent to tell him the terrible news?

'They think she's going to make it.'

'Thank God.' The hot tears welled up in his eyes and he could have embraced Grant, but didn't. Instead,

166

Boyd gazed at her searchingly, praying she wasn't lying, while hopeful relief flowed over him like a warm tide.

'Let's walk,' she said. 'I've got a car parked a couple of streets away.'

'That's wonderful news,' said Boyd. 'What did they say about her?'

'It's early days.' She seemed amazingly young and vulnerable, with auburn hair and an oval face with a rather muddy complexion. She wore jeans and a sweatshirt.

'Is she conscious?'

'Not while I was there. But she's breathing on her own. They took her off the respirator.'

'I didn't know she was on a respirator. They wouldn't tell me a thing.' Boyd's hopes rose, but suppose Grant wasn't a police officer after all? Suppose she was leading him to his assassin, or Grant *was* his assassin? 'I need to see your ID,' he said.

'Of course,' replied Grant. 'I should have showed it to you.' She had her police ID in the palm of her hand. But the ID could so easily have been forged. Again the labyrinth closed in on the fanciful Boyd. For a minute he could almost hear the roar of the Minotaur.

'I'm going to be shadowing you all the time now while you're outside Aston. But I don't want to cramp your style – or disrupt your investigation.'

'The shadow shadowed,' said Boyd.

'What are you planning to do after the hospital visit?'

'I'm going to have a chat with Bill Farley, one of the prison officers I met on A Wing.'

'Where?'

'The Rising Sun in Yardley Street.'

'I'll call a colleague and we'll go there too, but we'll stay as far away from you as possible.'

'Are you armed?'

'Yes.'

'Are there any developments in the CID investigation?'

'All the prison officers on the unit are being reinterviewed – including Farley. You'll be seen tomorrow.'

They reached her car – a Vauxhall Cavalier – and she
drove him to the hospital. During the journey, Boyd
said, 'Do you think we're being followed?'

Lucy was casually looking into her rear mirror. 'Not at
the moment.'

'You've done a lot of this kind of work?'

'What are you trying to say? That you'd rather have a
bloke?'

'Not at all,' said Boyd glibly and then felt uncomfortable.

'Stop worrying,' she said. 'You haven't offended me.
I have to handle that kind of prejudice all the time.' She
didn't sound bitter.

'Do you know about this case?'

'No. I don't need to know any details. All the information I have is that you're a police officer working undercover who ran into trouble.'

'You know what happened last night?'

'That's all I've been given. I'm very sorry about your
fiancée. That's why I went to check her out for you.'

'I'm grateful.'

'It's the least I could have done for you.'

Suddenly Boyd began to like WPC Grant a whole lot
more.

Twenty minutes later WPC Grant and Boyd were walking along the wide corridor towards the ward. The walls
were hung with a set of depressing watercolours, showing idealised landscapes. There was a hint of heavenly
grace in the landscapes with golden light and an
unearthly glow.

'So who do I pass you off as?'

'I'm your sister.'

'Thank you for telling me. I sometimes get confused.'

*   *   *

168

'She's conscious and breathing naturally,' said the nurse. 'Came off the respirator an hour ago.'

'What can you tell me?'

'She's very –'

'Poorly?'

'Yes.' The nurse looked flustered.

She led the way to the side room where a uniformed police officer sat. Lucy Grant pulled up a chair and sat down beside him. Neither spoke.

Between the three of us, thought Boyd, we're providing quite a police presence here. The officer nodded at him as Boyd went over to stand beside Marcia, who was wired up to drips and high tech monitoring equipment.

Her eyes were closed.

Boyd sat down on a chair beside the bed and took her hand. 'It's Danny,' he whispered.

Marcia opened her eyes and at first there was no recognition in them. Then she seemed afraid.

'I love you,' he said.

Her lips moved, but no sound came out.

'You're going to be all right.'

She closed her eyes again as if she didn't believe him.

They were silent for some time.

Then Marcia gave a little whimper. 'Hurts,' she muttered.

'Are you in pain? Shall I call a nurse?'

Marcia shook her head. 'Bother,' she said.

'It isn't a bother.'

'Hurts.'

Boyd pressed the button on the wall and a bell rang in the distance. Almost immediately the nurse arrived.

'She says she's in pain.'

'I'll give her some relief.'

'What kind of relief?'

'Morphine.'

He nodded. 'Can I stay?'

'I don't think so. Come again soon.'

'OK.' Boyd leant over Marcia and kissed her on the forehead. 'I'll be back later.'

'Soon,' she muttered, closing her eyes again.

'Very soon.'

Boyd left the side room and saw Lucy Grant talking to a young man in plain clothes. There could be no doubt that he was yet another police officer. How many more were there to come? wondered Boyd. Would they soon fill the corridor?

WPC Grant gazed down at her watch. 'Time for your next appointment,' she said, and gave Boyd a meaningful glance.

'So you're often on this kind of duty?' asked Boyd as Grant drove him towards the Rising Sun through a network of narrow streets. She drove with precision, never seeming to make a mistake.

'Yes. I get a lot of this kind of thing.'

'Any special qualifications?'

'I'm a good shot,' she said. 'And I know London.'

'How's that?'

'I used to be a cab driver.'

Boyd closed his eyes and leaned back, seeing Marcia wired up in her hospital bed.

'I'm really sorry about your friend.'

'She got shot by a bullet that was meant for me. Like a complete fool I went to her flat last night, seeking safety after they tried to kill me.'

'Your job's hazardous,' said WPC Grant. 'And the same hazards apply to anyone who's close to you.'

'That's why I'm going to resign.'

'You'll be missed.' She spoke reassuringly, as if he was a troubled child.

'For God's sake –'

'Your reputation travels before you.'

'That's rather unfortunate for an undercover officer.'

'I was told you were one of the best.'

'Were you now.' Boyd changed the subject hurriedly.

He only needed reassurance about Marcia. 'I'm terrified she's going to die.'

'If she survived the operating theatre, she's got a good chance.'

'She's the reason I want to resign.'

'You going to live together?'

'Please God.'

'Keep praying,' said WPC Grant as she deftly turned a corner.

'Are you a believer?'

'Yes. I always have been. In fact I'm a deacon at our local church.'

'Taxi driver. Deacon. WPC. What next?'

'Not a lot. Do *you* believe in prayer?'

'I used to pray as a child. "Gentle Jesus, meek and mild, Look upon a little child . . ." I believed he did.'

'What stopped you believing?'

'Life.'

'I'll put your friend on my prayer list.'

'Thank you,' said Boyd. Suddenly, strangely, he felt more hopeful.

The Rising Sun was scruffy and run-down and there was a lot of noise from the snooker table across the counter in the other bar.

WPC Grant and her colleague were sitting at a table for two, talking animatedly and roaring with laughter. They looked very convincing.

Soon Farley was walking towards him, hand out-stretched, apologising for being late and then going back to the bar to replenish Boyd's whisky and get a large one for himself. I'm not meant to touch alcohol, thought Boyd. The dry-out was in vain. Then he laughed.

'Private joke?' asked Farley. 'Or can I share it?'

Boyd struggled for a reply and eventually said, 'I went on the wagon recently. I shouldn't be drinking.'

'Did you have a problem?'

'Not really,' Boyd lied. 'I just wanted to see what the world was like without alcohol.'

'And what *was* it like?'

'Bleak.'

'Well?' asked Farley. His speech was slightly slurred and Boyd realised he'd already been drinking. 'And what about the rest of the world outside A Wing?'

'I don't think I can stick it.'

'Hathaway's experiment is over.'

'It's been deliberately sabotaged.'

Farley nodded and there was a long silence. Boyd didn't want to break it, but in the end he felt he had to turn the conversation into a subtle interrogation – something he didn't seem to be very good at doing, judging from past experience.

'I was very taken with Rhodes,' he began.

'He's an incredibly dangerous man.'

Farley's reaction was unexpected and out of keeping with his previous conversation in the prison canteen, and Boyd was a little thrown. 'So Broadmoor is the right place?'

'Providing they allow his writing and his research to continue, yes.'

'Surely he won't find anyone as supportive as you . . .'

Farley seemed reluctant to comment.

'When are you retiring?'

Farley obviously found this a more acceptable question. 'As soon as they let me go – maybe at the end of the month.'

'Are you still going on that cruise?'

'I don't know. Liz is the centre of my world. She won't be able to join me on a cruise.'

'Does she live with you?'

'She's got her own flat. How about you? Do you see your kids now you're divorced?' Farley seemed to be firmly side-stepping.

'We didn't have any, but I'm in a new relationship.'

'Is she the friend with cancer?'

'Yes.'

'Shouldn't you be with her?'

'I've just seen her.'

'How is she today?' Farley seemed full of sympathetic interest.

'OK.'

'You sure?'

'No worse.'

'Not better?'

'Not really.' Boyd wondered why Farley was pressing him so hard.

'I hope to God she'll be all right. My brother's wife died of cancer.'

'I'm very sorry.'

Farley said nothing. Feeling increasingly agitated, Boyd went to the bar and replenished their glasses, making sure he bought doubles. He might as well capitalise on Farley's intake. But what about his own? Abstinence had given him a poor head for the stuff.

But when Boyd returned, Farley seemed even more distant.

'How did you get on with Jones and Royston?'

'I didn't.'

Boyd laughed and then wished he hadn't.

'All I do know,' said Farley, 'is that Aidan Jones was the biggest bastard of the lot.'

Boyd felt that something significant was being said, but in a foreign language he couldn't understand. He also felt light-headed and cursed his weakness about the whisky.

'How do you make that out?'

'He was an animal.' Farley was looking into an empty glass. 'Come on. Let's have another one – or are you driving?'

'No.'

'You got a flat round here?'

'Just a bedsit, until I can get somewhere decent.' Boyd decided to take the risk, hoping he'd be able to get away from him when they left the pub.

173

As he returned from the bar, Farley seemed to be staring at Lucy Grant and her colleague and at first Boyd felt unnerved. Then he realised he was simply staring ahead.

'Why do you think Jones was more of a bastard than the others?' Giving Lucy what he hoped was a casual glance. Boyd noticed she was talking into a mobile – and there was an urgency that made him wary.

Farley stopped staring at Lucy and turned his blank gaze on Boyd. 'He didn't suffer from any remorse at all.'

'Did the others?'

'I suppose not.' Farley sounded impatient. He took a sip of his whisky and then went off at a tangent. 'I'm increasingly coming round to the conspiracy theory. It wouldn't be that difficult to operate.'

'Doesn't every prison officer's background get checked out?' asked Boyd.

'Easy enough to build up a false one – even easier if you've got the right connections.'

'How would they have been recruited?'

'Hand-picked, probably. Men who were prepared to be long-term main chancers if they were well compensated.'

'So do you think A Wing is only part of the operation?'

'It could be. What about another drink?'

Boyd agreed, trying not to sound reluctant. He knew he would have to make this his last. While Farley was at the bar he wondered what had happened to make him dislike Jones so much.

'So the conspiracy theory still holds for you?' he said when they were both drinking again.

'Yes. Maybe their next task is to spring the Maxtons.' But Farley seemed distracted and uninterested in the possibility.

'Is it *so* important to get the Maxtons out?'

'The Maxton brothers are very bad news. They're responsible for drug trafficking, protection, and a lot of

174

serious crime in South London. They're worth a lot of money, and I mean a *lot* of money.'

'What happens if they're sprung?'

'They'll probably go abroad. They've already got links with some of the drug cartels in South America and a lot depends on them being free. It's all economics.'

'What do you think the chances are?'

'Good,' said Farley. 'Still good, despite what we know. We need to be on the alert.' He drank his whisky and got up. 'I must be getting home. I get these terrible migraines . . .'

'So I hear.'

'And if I don't have a good night's sleep I'm up shit creek.'

They shook hands and then, to Boyd's amazement, Farley began to walk a little unsteadily towards Lucy and her colleague, both of whom were talking as animatedly as before.

He brushed past them in the crowd and Boyd felt relieved.

Then Farley turned back, paused by Grant's side and said something to her.

As he strode towards the door of the Rising Sun, Boyd noticed he was much steadier on his feet.

Boyd paused. What the hell had Farley said to Lucy? Why had he stopped and spoken to her at all? He went to the toilet and as he stood by the urinal his pessimism returned, followed by acute anxiety.

Chapter Twelve

The Rising Sun, Yardley Street
23 June 2001 – 2230 hours

When Boyd returned, WPC Grant had gone and he went out into the street to look for her. There was the gentle patter of rain and the pavements glistened as she emerged from behind a parked truck.

'He's gone,' she said.

'What the hell did he say to you?'

'He wondered where the Fox and Grapes was. I'm afraid we couldn't direct him.'

'Why didn't he ask me?'

'Maybe because he thought you wouldn't know.'

'He must have changed his mind. He said he was going home.'

'People do it all the time. Especially when they've had a lot to drink.'

'I still find Farley's behaviour very odd,' said Boyd. 'That of all the people in the saloon bar he should pick on you. He could have asked anyone.'

Grant shrugged. 'Maybe I look helpful.' She didn't seem concerned.

'Maybe you looked like a plain-clothes police officer.'

'Now you're being paranoid.'

'I hope so.' Boyd paused and then said, 'I need to see Marcia again.'

'You have to go to a safe house for the night.'

'You're going to drive me?'

'That's the idea.'

Boyd looked around him, but the street was almost deserted.

WPC Grant then said, 'I'm very concerned about this hospital visit.'

'Why?'

'Your movements are getting predictable.'

'You mean we're being followed?'

'It's a possibility.'

'You've seen them?'

'No.'

'Anything suspicious?'

'No. But I'd rather you went straight to the safe house tonight. I don't want to take any risks.'

'I'm sorry,' said Boyd. 'I've got to see her. I've got to find out how she's getting on.'

Grant paused. 'Can't you phone?'

'No.'

'Look, I've got something to tell you.'

'Is Marcia –' Boyd was instantly facing the worst.

'It's got nothing to do with your friend.'

'What then?'

'Let's drive and I'll tell you as we go. What I want you to do is to get into the car and lie on the floor at the back. I realise conditions will be a little cramped.'

WPC Grant drove with her usual professionalism and Boyd, lying on the floor in the back of the car, was sure she was continually checking, wondering if they were being followed. Then she said, 'We found something out about Farley – or at least CID did. They need to double-check, but I think you should know.'

'Know what?'

'Farley changed his name a few years ago.'

'Why?'

'Because his wife Lydia Stevens was one of Aidan Jones's victims. He raped and then strangled her.'

'For God's sake . . .' Boyd's thoughts were racing and

177

he felt slightly sick. 'Farley said he was divorced. When did this happen?'

'About five years ago.'

'Why did he change his name?'

'They don't know.'

Boyd felt stunned and left out of the investigation that was being carried out behind his back. 'Why the hell wasn't I told?'

'Because they've only just found out. Apparently.'

'Was that the call you were taking in the pub?'

'Yes. It was rather nerve-racking – especially when you were talking to Farley. Did he say anything useful to you?'

'He did appear to loathe Aidan Jones in particular. He called him an animal.'

'Do you think that Farley was approached, and grabbed a golden opportunity for revenge – or could he be working on his own?'

'There must be others involved,' said Boyd. 'It wasn't Farley who attacked me at the takeaway or shot Marcia.' He tried to stay calm, but he felt as if the whole investigation was escalating away from him and was now in the hands of others.

Then he tried to damp down his indignation. Lennox had had the advantage of interviewing each officer, maybe two or even three times. How could he ever have done that? He was an insider, like all the others, except that he was working for the opposite side. Boyd had never had competition like this in his previous under-cover jobs.

'Shit!' he said aloud.

Grant sighed. 'I don't think it's a good idea to take all this personally.'

'What am I meant to do? I'm completely redundant. I had to move too fast, they know who I am and that's why you're protecting me. I would imagine that every one of those implants knows who I really am.'

'I don't think that's how they work. They're not kept in touch with current developments. Why should they

178

be? They've been planted and have various objectives. Right now they're moving towards Plan B. The infiltrators probably work in cells – each one's only given the most limited possible information.'

'So how did Lennox get the information about Farley?'

'I told you – I don't know. But going on guesswork I would think they'd run each of the victims' families and friends through the computer to see what they came up with. So at last you've made progress – even if the progress had nothing to do with you.'

'I'm not a team player,' said Boyd.

'You are now.'

'In fact I would have thought my usefulness was over.'

'I don't think so.'

'Why not?'

'Because you're a target.'

'You mean I'll continue to draw their fire. Is that all I'm worth?'

'It's quite something,' said Grant patiently. 'While they still want to kill you, you're useful.'

'Thanks a bunch,' said Boyd. He paused. Grant seemed to be driving very slowly and he was consumed by agitation. 'How far to the hospital now?'

'Couldn't you call them?'

'I want to see her.'

'You realise that increases the danger?'

'I must see her.'

'OK.' She gave in, but Boyd was sure she was acting against her better judgement. So was he. But Marcia was now his only real concern.

When Boyd arrived, she seemed to be in much the same condition as before, eyes closed, wired up, barely alive.

There was no sign of a nurse or the attendant police officer as Boyd sat down beside Marcia and took her hand. Then he realised she was breathing raggedly, with an ominous rattling sound, and she didn't respond to him at all.

Boyd got up and went in search of help, his heart pounding. How could she have deteriorated so fast?

Eventually he was able to locate the staff nurse.

'Miss Williams's breathing is bad and she doesn't respond when I squeeze her hand.'

'Are you a relation?'

Boyd almost lost control. Surely to God they couldn't be going through this routine again. 'I'm going to marry her,' he said in despair.

'Unfortunately she picked up an infection, and as a result she's –'

'Poorly?' Boyd supplied the magic word.

'Yes.'

'What are her chances?'

'I can't tell you that. But the night duty doctor will be around.'

'I'll wait for him.'

'He could be some time.'

'I said I'll wait. I'm going to wait right here. Do you get me?'

'Very well.' The nurse walked away.

Suddenly he heard the sound of sirens approaching the hospital. Then they were switched off. Boyd looked out of the window and saw flashing blue lights in the car park, but paid little attention.

About twenty minutes later, the doctor arrived, middle-aged and in a hurry. He brushed past Boyd on his way into Marcia's room. Deeply apprehensive, Boyd paced up and down, waiting to pounce on him as he went off, moving aside to make room for a hospital porter pushing a woman in a wheelchair. He glanced at Boyd with a mixture of agitation and rather melodramatic importance – as if he was desperate to communicate.

'Shocking business,' he said.

'Eh?' Boyd gazed at him, thoughts elsewhere.

180

'Outside. In the car park.'

'What?'

'Young woman. Shot in her car.'

'Is she all right?'

'She got shot through the head,' the porter said over his shoulder as he continued on down the corridor, pushing the wheelchair at considerable speed.

Boyd felt as if he had suddenly received a hard physical blow. If anything had happened to Grant it was his fault. They'd have been at the safe house now if he hadn't insisted on coming to the hospital. But maybe the shooting had nothing to do with her, nothing to do with him after all. Nevertheless, whatever had happened outside, he still had to check on Marcia.

Unable to wait any longer, Boyd pushed open the door of her side room to see the doctor adjusting a tube that went into a hole in her throat.

'Excuse me.'

'Yes?' The kind Indian face was solemn and because of that solemnity oddly comforting. Behind him, Marcia was still making the rattling sound.

'Miss Williams – I'm going to – we're going to be married. I *must* know how she is. Really must know.'

'Of course.' He laid a hand on Boyd's arm and steered him out of the side room and into an empty nurses' office. He sat down and invited Boyd to join him on a cracked leather sofa. For a moment the doctor was silent and Boyd waited apprehensively. Then he said, 'I have to tell you she is a very sick lady.'

'Will she live?'

'I'm pumping her full of antibiotics. It's easy to pick up an infection in a hospital, especially when the patient's so weak.'

'The bullet went into her chest.'

'Fortunately the trajectory just missed her heart. The bullet was removed successfully and we thought her chances were good.'

'And now?'

'She is very ill again.'

'Can I see her?'

'Of course.'

'Will she get better?' Boyd persisted, desperately trying to force an assurance out of him.

The doctor settled back on the sofa as if he had all the time in the world. 'There is only a slim chance,' he admitted. 'I'm sorry. We shall do our best.' He got up and stood over Boyd for a while. 'As I say, there is a chance. She is being very carefully monitored.'

'Thank you for being honest with me.'

Fleetingly the Indian doctor gripped Boyd's shoulder and then slowly left the office.

Boyd stayed where he was, unable to cope with the shock of Marcia's deterioration. She had been his victim, and if anything had happened to Lucy Grant then she was another victim, someone he had dragged into the tentacles.

After a few minutes, a young nurse poked her head round the office door. 'There's a DI Lennox who wants to see you, Mr Taylor.' The nurse looked anxious.

'I don't want to see him.'

'He's coming up.'

Boyd got off the sofa, pushed past her and ran for a lift. 'And I'm going down.'

The car park was still a mass of flashing blue lights as Boyd cautiously left the hospital. He tried to walk slowly and casually as he returned to WPC Grant's car. But he couldn't get near. Then he saw a security man from the hospital.

'What's happened?'

'Young woman – shot through the head. Hell of a mess.'

'She's dead?'

'You bet she is.'

Boyd felt sick. This could have been avoided if only

182

he'd gone to the safe house and not forced Grant to take him to Marcia.

Boyd made a decision. Protection would be replaced. Lennox was no doubt searching for him now, but he wanted to be on his own, to duck and dive, not allow anyone else to be a victim. His victim.

He decided to take a taxi from the rank outside the hospital. As he waited and the vehicle began to move towards him, Boyd felt not the slightest hint of fear – only a deep despair that was all-pervasive.

As he was driven through the darkened streets, Boyd looked out of the rear window but couldn't make out any sign of pursuit, but then he hadn't earlier and they'd been there. He turned back to watch the cabbie, a burly Afro-Caribbean who was driving slowly, as if he had all the time in the world.

'Can you speed up a bit?' asked Boyd.

'You in a hurry?'

'I want to get there tonight.'

'I can't break the speed limit. It's more than my licence is worth.'

'OK.' Boyd sat back in his seat and closed his eyes. All he wanted to do was sleep. The effect of the whisky was giving him a numbness, a detachment for which he was grateful.

'You all right, sir?'

'Just tired.'

'You been to the hospital for your heart?'

It was a curious question. 'No. I went to see a patient, a friend of mine.'

'Is she better?'

'She's worse.'

'I'm sorry.'

'She's got an infection.'

'That was her illness? An infection?'

'No – she was very ill before. She caught an infection.'

'Miracles can happen if you pray, sir. Really pray hard enough.'

What a coincidence, thought Boyd. A religious lecture.

183

But maybe I should be praying, he thought suddenly, remembering the faith of Lucy Grant.

'You believe?'

'In God? Yes, sir. I do believe in God. Do you?'

'I've never really thought about it.' Boyd's numbness was wearing off and he began to shake, folding his arms, trying to keep himself still.

'You start praying. You really start praying.'

'And something will happen?'

'Prayers are answered. But not always how we want them answered.' He paused. 'What is the number, sir?'

Boyd suddenly realised they were driving down the terraced street where Bill Farley lived.

'It's number 14.'

The cab slowed down and Boyd got out, giving the cabbie a substantial tip.

'Thank you, sir. That's generous.'

'Pray for her,' said Boyd.

'What's her name?'

'Marcia.'

'OK, sir. I'll pray for Marcia.'

Boyd rang the bell, but there was no reply and he pressed it again, listening to the shrilling in the house, wondering if Farley was still out or too drunk to reply. He pushed open the letterbox, but could only see a small patch of carpet. Then he saw two very small feet.

The door was opened on its chain.

'Who is it?'

'I'm Luke Taylor. One of Bill Farley's colleagues from the prison. I need to speak to him urgently.'

'My father's gone away.'

'Where?'

'I don't know.' She sounded scared.

'Can I come in?'

'I don't know you.'

'I'm a prison officer.'

She made a sudden decision, unbolted the door and opened it wide, looking up at Boyd in nervous expectation. She was the girl he had seen in Farley's bed. His daughter.

She looked up at him. 'I can't think where he's gone.'

'I've only just seen him,' said Boyd gently.

'He came home.'

'When?'

'Just now.' She looked at her watch. 'About ten minutes ago. He said he was going away.'

'I don't understand.'

'Neither do I.' She was close to tears. 'What do you want with him?'

'Just a talk.'

'About the prison?'

'Yes.'

'But you said you'd been with him. Haven't you already talked? And what's the urgency?'

'I had an idea.'

'What about?'

'Something to do with work.'

'Is there more trouble?'

Boyd decided to be direct. 'There's been a lot of trouble.'

'Those men –'

'The murders.'

She suddenly began to cry and Boyd, without even thinking, put his arms around her. Her tears turned to a harsh, dry sobbing. Then she pulled away.

'My father was drunk,' she said. 'I didn't know what to do.'

She led Boyd into the sitting room and they sat down on the sofa.

'He'd been drinking before we met. Do you know what's the matter with him?'

She shook her head, but Boyd was sure she knew something.

'Where's he gone?'

185

She stared at him blankly.

'I don't know your name,' he lied.

'It's Liz.'

'Look, Liz, you've got to tell me everything you know. I don't want your dad to be exposed to any danger.'

'I don't know what's going on –'

'Has he got a place to go to?'

'Not that I know of.'

Boyd stared at her, his nerves screaming. Should he tell her that he knew about her mother or not? He could totally scare her off – or he might get Liz to co-operate. It was an impossible decision and an appalling risk.

'I know about your mother.'

'What about her?'

'I know how she died.'

'Yes.' Liz sounded almost relieved. 'Who told you?'

'Your father.' It was hard to lie to her, but he saw no alternative.

'*He* told you?'

'Yes.'

'That's unlikely.'

'But true.'

'He never even told Mr Brand, so why should he tell you?' She was more astute than he had imagined and suddenly Boyd had his back to the wall.

'He was – I'm afraid he was very drunk. He's obviously been very unhappy over the last few days. He was put in charge of training me and we just got close. You know how it is – some people you instantly click with, others you don't.'

'What did he tell you?'

Boyd felt increasingly unsure of himself.

'He told me that your mother was raped and strangled.' A wave of self-loathing swept him. If she didn't know, he would be hurting her cruelly. Then he saw the understanding in her eyes. 'You did know that?'

She nodded. 'But there's something else, isn't there?' she said. 'Tell me about that.'

What was she doing? Testing him out in some way? Boyd's panic returned and he hesitated.

'You can tell me,' she persisted, and Boyd had the uncanny feeling that she had got the upper hand.

'OK – the man who murdered your mother was a serial killer.'

'And his name?'

'Aidan Jones. He was on A wing at Aston.'

She nodded again.

'And your dad changed his name from Stevens to Farley.'

'He wanted to kill him,' she said. 'He always wanted to kill him – and he was with this horrible man every day.'

'And now Jones is dead.'

She nodded yet again, her expression inscrutable.

There was a silence which Boyd eventually broke.

'Did you know he was going to kill him?'

'I didn't know about Jones until the press reported his death. I didn't even know he was in Aston. When I found out I pleaded with Dad to tell me what happened.'

'What did he say?'

'That it was all a coincidence. That he never touched him.'

'Did you believe that?'

'At first.'

'But not now?'

'No. At least I don't know. Can you tell me?'

'No. I'm afraid I can't.'

'He didn't confide in you?'

'Absolutely not. But, tell me, why did he change his name?'

'Dad told me that he wanted to make a fresh start – to get away from what had happened.'

'But a fresh start while still a prison officer seems strange.'

'Dad had always felt relationships between prisoners

187

and warders were important. He didn't want to give up the job – he needed to feel he was helping people.'

'Presumably he didn't want to help Aidan Jones,' said Boyd drily.

Liz stared at him. 'After Mum died, well, after the trial, he said that he'd been dreaming of killing Jones.'

'By that stage Jones had been in prison for over a year –'

'Not in my dad's prison. At least, not then. I don't suppose he thought they'd end up together on the lifers' wing. It was terribly ironic.'

'And dangerous.'

'Yes.' She looked away. 'You think Dad killed him?'

'I don't know. What did you think?'

'Deep inside. I couldn't help thinking it was a possibility. I tried to bury the idea, but it kept coming back.' She paused. 'Especially since Dad started drinking heavily.'

'I've got to find him fast.'

She gave Boyd a curious look. 'You seem to be very involved in all this.'

Boyd knew he had to be careful. 'Yes. I do feel very involved. I don't know your father well, but I like and admire him and his attitude to the prisoners is compassionate. He's working with one – a man called Rhodes – who seems disturbed and is being transferred to Broadmoor. Did your father ever talk about him?'

'No. He never talks about his work, and I don't ask him. It's a kind of unspoken rule which we both obey.'

'What do you talk about?'

'Mum – a lot. I'm studying to be a drama teacher but I haven't been that well. We talk a lot about that too.'

'He said you'd been having hormone treatment.'

'For growth, yes. I've always been small, but my doctor thought this particular treatment really would work. It isn't.'

'So you share a lot with your father?'

'We both have our ways of survival. I have my studies

188

– and a few friends,' she added sadly 'But I think a lot about my mother. She was coming home late from work and that revolting man followed her down this alley and – then it all happened.'

'And your father – how does he spend his spare time?'

'He's got very interested in history. He belongs to a club that visits historical sites and is always reading and borrowing books from the library.'

'Did you know that Rhodes was writing a history of the English-speaking peoples?'

'I knew a prisoner was doing something of the kind, and Dad was helping him, but I didn't know his name. He really does care for the inmates though.' She paused, looking worried. 'But the terrible coincidence of Jones –'

'Hardly a coincidence. Your father must have known he was there.'

She was impatient. 'He didn't apply to be on the lifers' wing. They transferred him there.'

'And no one had any knowledge of the connection?'

'I'm sure they didn't. Dad had changed his name and everything.'

'Who's he closest to – amongst the officers?'

'He never talked about any of them except Ted Brand. He seemed to like him. I believe he's in charge of A Wing.'

'Do you think Brand would know where he's gone?'

'He might, I suppose.' She seemed doubtful.

Boyd got up. 'I'm sorry if I seem to be cross-examining you. I was with your dad for a long time tonight and I want to help him.'

'Do *you* know why he's gone off like this?'

'We met to discuss the closure of the lifers' wing. Did he mention that to you at all?' Boyd risked his last question, but she shrugged. 'Didn't he tell you he planned to retire?'

189

She shook her head. 'I told you, we never discuss his work. Don't you believe me?'

'Of course I believe you. I'll try to get hold of Brand.'

In fact Boyd had no intention of contacting him. He still needed to avoid police protection and stay near Marcia. Maybe he should simply sleep in a hospital corridor. Would the police find him there? Or the Syndicate? Suppose Farley had been operating alone? Having waited for his moment, could he have killed them all? Suppose there *was* no conspiracy? Suppose there *was* no infiltration? But how could Farley have murdered three men on his own in a secure unit with continuous CCTV surveillance?

Surely logic dictated that a large organisation was involved. Otherwise he wouldn't have had the attempt made on his life at the takeaway, Marcia wouldn't have got shot, and neither would WPC Lucy Grant. But who made the cogs turn so viciously still remained a mystery.

'Are you going to be all right on your own?' asked Boyd.

'Of course I am.'

'Can I phone you later to see if your father's made contact?'

'Of course.' She got up, went over to a desk and wrote down the telephone number. 'I shan't be sleeping.'

'Meanwhile – take care of yourself.'

Liz looked up at him, her small body poised, a child waiting for a kiss. To his own surprise, Boyd hugged her again.

'We'll keep in touch.'

'I need help,' she said.

'I know that. I'll do all I can.'

As he left and hurried through the empty streets, Boyd

190

was sure he was being followed. Farley's house must have been under surveillance and they would have seen him and were probably closing in. Then he saw the taxi and ran towards the vehicle which was cruising slowly along the road.

'Where to?'

Boyd paused with one hand on the handle of the door.

'Wait a minute.' Of course, the cruising cab *had* to be theirs. 'No.'

'Eh?'

'I'm sorry. I've just remembered.'

'Just remembered what?' The driver was scowling at him.

'I don't need you after all.'

'Why don't you make up your bleedin' mind?' The cab accelerated away and Boyd, now running in sweat, strode along the street, feeling completely vulnerable to the sluggish night traffic, flinching as a Rover kerb-crawled, breaking into a run as another cab driver drew up behind.

Boyd felt the labyrinth closing in around him. Who knows how many personnel they had deployed? The Syndicate could have hired anyone, including Farley and Brand. He stood no chance against them and all he could do was return to the hospital where he was still exposed and vulnerable, but might stand more of a chance. How could he have ever imagined for one moment that Farley was a lone operator?

Marcia had to live. She was his only hope of a future and she was now like a frail moth heading for the electric light, soon to be frazzled into nothing. How was he going to bear his arid life if she died?

Boyd knew he would be alone again, changing identity, plunging into case after case, eventually, hopefully, dying himself in some conflict when his apparently charmed life finally ran out of luck.

'Excuse me.'

191

Boyd gasped as a small white van drew up at the kerb beside him. He didn't stop walking and the van followed.

'Excuse me.' The woman was leaning out of the window with something in her hand.

Boyd broke into a run.

But the driver was persistent and began to shout at him.

'Do you know where Newbolt Street is?' the woman yelled.

Boyd felt frozen, unable to move, and the small white van caught up with him.

This is it, he thought.

'Newbolt Street? I've been driving round for hours and I can't find Newbolt Street.' She was elderly, looking up at him hopefully.

'Newbolt Street,' Boyd repeated, wondering if her van had been hijacked and there was someone with a gun in the back.

'Yes.' The elderly woman was getting impatient. 'I can't find Newbolt Street.'

'I'm sorry. I'm a stranger here. There's a late-night coffee stall down the road. They'll know.'

'Thank you.' She drove away, but as she did so her battered vehicle backfired and Boyd flung himself on to the ground, rolling over, much to the amusement of a gang of youths who were staggering drunkenly out of a club.

Boyd rolled over yet again, coming hard up against the shopfront of an off-licence and cracking his head against a concrete post.

'This guy's pissed out of his mind,' said one of the youths. 'Totally rat-arsed.'

Boyd looked up at the group as they surrounded him. He staggered to his feet. 'Why don't you all fuck off?'

'What do you want?' asked another of the group. 'A good kicking?'

Boyd began to run and they gave chase, whooping

and cheering and shouting obscenities. As he easily outstripped them, he raced for the hospital, realising that the pursuit meant safety, for while the gang of youths were after him, he would need no further protection.

Chapter Thirteen

South London Hospital
24 June 2001 – 0400 hours

'She's very poorly.'

Boyd stood staring at the nurse incredulously, sweating profusely. She couldn't be using the tired words again. But she was.

'I need to see her.'

Again the nurse was a stranger to him.

'I'm afraid –'

Boyd pushed past her, heading for the side room, determined that no one would stop him. He opened the door and saw Marcia, lying on her back, gasping for breath.

He knew she was dying.

A nurse was adjusting the drip and another was holding her hand.

'I'm her fiancé,' he whispered. 'I need to be with her.'

'She's slipping away,' said the nurse. She spoke too loudly and Boyd put a finger to his lips, as if there was a spell to be broken.

'No,' he said vehemently. But the emptiness was already there, the knowledge that there was nothing more he could do and the inevitable had to happen.

He sat down beside Marcia and took her hand, raising it to his lips and kissing her clammy palm. Boyd looked up to see her lips were moving.

Then she spoke, bringing the words out in gasps. 'The angel of mercy,' she rasped.

'She'll come,' said Boyd, responding instinctively.

'She's here.'

'I'm glad.'

'She's very small. She's on a Christmas tree. Mum always puts her up there. The Christmas angel.'

'How small?'

'Oh, very small indeed. She'd fit in your pocket.'

Something blazed across the inner recesses of Boyd's mind. Something important. In a flash it was gone – as if a code had been cracked but the meaning lost.

'It's me. Danny.'

'I know.'

'We've got a future.'

She smiled and her lips began to move again, but no sound came out.

Marcia was still smiling, but she didn't blink. There was a small rattling sound, almost like the clearing of a throat. Boyd bent over her, but her eyes were sightlessly staring up at him.

'She's gone,' whispered the nurse.

'No,' muttered Boyd. 'For Christ's sake – no.'

'I'm sorry.' The nurse wrote down something in her log.

'Can't you get her back?'

'No.'

'Call the crash team?'

'She's dead,' said the other nurse. 'It was the infection. I'll call the doctor, of course.'

Boyd remained in the chair at Marcia's side. 'There was a future,' he said brokenly, but he knew he was like a child crying at the dying of the light.

Death had come again. The tears came, running down Boyd's face as he sat there, holding Marcia's hand.

The young houseman arrived in a flurry and pronounced Marcia dead. There was no sign of the Indian doctor and Boyd was disappointed.

'Are you family?' the houseman asked, looking at his watch.

'I'm her fiancé.'

'I'm sorry,' he mumbled. 'Who is her next of kin?'

'Her sister.'

'Has she been told?'

'No. I don't know where she lives.' Again the phrase blazed across his mind. *She's very small.* And so she was, Boyd thought. *She'd fit in your pocket.* Marcia was right – she'd fit anywhere. Suddenly Boyd had a solution that was so simple he could hardly believe he had arrived at the understanding at last. Then his grief flooded back and he gazed down at Marcia, seeing the smile a rictus on her face. She died with a smile on her face. That phrase seemed like a parody, or a cliché that Marcia would have enjoyed.

The doctor was looking at him impatiently and Boyd realised he must have said something he hadn't heard.

'I'm sorry?'

'How can we get hold of her sister?'

Boyd walked away. 'I told you – I've absolutely no idea.'

'But you must –'

The young doctor's voice was lost in the slamming of the door.

Boyd hurried down the corridor. The solution had a simplicity that was almost perfect as Boyd remembered Marcia's dying words. *Oh, very small indeed. She'd fit in your pocket.*

'Thank you,' he whispered.

She had unwittingly activated the part of his mind that had remained closed to the other option, the simplest of all solutions. What a waste of police time. He thought of WPC Lucy Grant. And above all, Marcia. What a fucking awful waste.

Of course, Marcia's killer would have been hired and

so had Grant's. Just a couple of hired hands – and they would have been readily available to anyone who had contact with criminal circles. Had he slowly put the money away from his salary? Slowly and steadily? Saving up? Putting the money into a piggy bank?

HM Prison Aston
24 June 2001 – 0700 hours

'I've got to see Mr Brand.'

'You can't go on A Wing,' said the duty officer over the intercom at the prison gate.

Boyd had taken a taxi and the driver had jokingly asked, 'Booking yourself in, are you?'

'I'm a prison officer,' Boyd had told him, as he ached for Marcia.

'Tough job,' the driver had said. 'Particularly at Aston. They bump the prisoners off there, don't they? I suppose that's expedient enough. Prevents overcrowding.'

Boyd hadn't been able to reply for he only saw Marcia's dead face. She'd given him hope. She'd also accidentally triggered a way forward. But he knew *his* only way forward was to plead with Creighton to get him back to work just as fast as he could.

Without Marcia he had nothing to live for. Why was everything always snatched away? He had nobody, so he would be nobody until Creighton gave him another identity. Then he'd plunge into the deadly game all over again. He would always be in danger and that would help to stop him remembering. And to be able to stop remembering was, and always would be, a glorious relief.

'Name and number?'

'Luke Taylor. 1630.'

'And you want to see Brand?'

'It's vital. I've got essential information about the A Wing killings. He has to see me. Immediately.'

'I'll try to speak to him. I don't even know if he's on shift.'

The duty officer was gone for what seemed like an eternity during which Boyd wept for Marcia and all their lost hopes.

'Luke Taylor?' crackled the intercom.

'Yes.'

'Mr Brand will see you now. I gather you're no longer working on A wing, so he's going to come and escort you. He says he hopes your visit is valid.'

'Very much so.'

'Wait here, please.'

The wait seemed interminable, but at last the gates opened and Brand's bulky figure stood there, waiting to be convinced.

'This had better be good,' he said.

Boyd nodded. 'You won't be disappointed.'

Brand and Boyd stood in the empty association area in A Wing, gazing up at the ventilation grilles.

Brand looked at him impatiently. 'You've talked yourself back into A Wing – on this kind of shit?'

'It's not shit. The person I'm thinking of would just fit the crawl space.'

'There *is* no space.'

'I disagree.' Boyd was insistent. 'The area extends over each pod –'

'Of course. It takes the air-conditioning.'

'So if someone was small enough to squeeze along the crawl space, providing they knew their way around, they could drop in on any of the lifers. With a knife. Let's go into one of the pods. How about Craig Royston's?'

Brand gazed at Boyd thoughtfully. 'You got someone in mind?'

'Yes.'

'Suppose you're right?'

'I think I am.'

198

'Rather blows apart the conspiracy theory. So maybe we're not riddled with insiders after all. That's a refreshing idea.'

'There was no conspiracy,' said Boyd. 'Not in the way we'd imagined.'

'OK,' said Brand. 'Let's go and take a look at the pod.'

'Have you got a ladder?' asked Boyd.

'This is where the killer got in.' Boyd climbed back down the ladder, allowing Brand to check for himself. 'You'll find the grille is very easily detachable.'

Boyd was in the toilet area of Craig Royston's pod, gazing up at Brand ascending the ladder to wrench at a grille in the plastic ceiling, revealing the small space that contained the air-conditioning.

'What are we talking about?' asked Brand derisively. 'One of the fairy folk?'

'No,' replied Boyd. 'Just a very small and rather fragile figure, neatly out of CCTV range. There must be a grille in all the pods in exactly the same position.'

'Of course there is. But you're on completely the wrong track. No one would fit the air-conditioning space.'

'The person I have in mind would fit, but only just,' said Boyd.

'But how would anyone know what direction to take?' demanded Brand. 'It must be like a maze up there.'

'There'll be a plan of the air-conditioning system with the original architect's drawings. And I don't imagine those drawings would be hard to get hold of and copy.'

'There's a set in the office,' admitted Brand.

'So your fairy was able to select a starting point and track a way through the air-conditioning space after carefully studying the plans and probably doing some reconnaissance.'

'Pity about the fairy being so obvious on camera when

she's climbed down from the grille and is in the bathroom area. And how is the little love going to climb
back?'

'By standing on the top of the lavatory cistern and
being agile,' said Boyd.

'But what *about* the cameras? You haven't answered
that question.'

'Suppose she hid behind the shower curtains?
Wouldn't that be an effective enough hiding place?
Enter the inmate who sits on the toilet, out of camera
range, and the fairy cuts his throat – also out of camera
range. Then she climbs up on to the top of the cistern
and disappears back into the crawl space. Dead easy. A
single operation with a little back-up. No infiltrators. No
mafiosi. No other insiders.'

'Your fairy would have to be very careful indeed. And
why are we using the word "she"?'

'I'll help you with that later. But you have to admit it's
a possibility.'

'Yes,' said Brand. 'It is. But what I don't understand is
how you got involved to this extent – how you ever
came up with this idea.'

'I'm a police undercover officer,' said Boyd baldly. 'So
sorry not to have told you before. I'm your insider and
there's only one of me.'

'For Christ's sake –'

'I'm afraid I don't carry any ID, but I'm sure you can
see why.'

Brand nodded. He seemed numbed. Then he said,
'Why did you run such a risk at that press conference?'

'At the time I thought there was fire to draw,' replied
Boyd. He paused and then said brokenly. 'And if I'd
only known what I know now I wouldn't have had to
do it. I thought we were up against a sophisticated
conspiracy with a lot of infiltrators. I was looking for
something too ambitious, too political, too far-ranging.
The operation was much simpler and on a much smaller
scale.'

Brand was staring at Boyd with deep concern. 'I don't understand,' he said.

'You will.'

'What are you going to do now?'

'Make an arrest.'

Boyd knocked on the door of the pretty terraced house. After a long delay it opened slowly. Liz Farley was wearing a dressing gown and looked incredibly young.

'Heard anything from your dad?' he asked.

'He hasn't come back.'

'Has he phoned?'

'No. I'm terribly worried about him. I still don't know what to do. Have you got any ideas?'

'I'm sorry.'

'Do you want to come in? I was just about to get up.'

'I did want to have a word.'

'I need company. I know it's early, but can I get you a drink, or a coffee?'

'No, thanks.' Boyd followed Liz into the sitting room and sat down on the sofa. She plunged into a big armchair and drew up her feet.

Then she stood up again and said restlessly, 'I need a drink myself.'

'Go ahead.'

Liz Farley went over to the sideboard where she poured herself a large scotch from a decanter and came and sat down opposite him again.

She sipped her scotch.

Boyd waited.

'Well?' she asked.

'It must have been so dreadful to lose your mother like that.'

Liz looked down at the floor.

'Why did your father wait for so long?'

201

'Wait for what?' She was growing tense, continually sipping at her whisky.

'Of course, he wanted to make it *look* like a conspiracy. I think that was clever. Presumably the only hired hands were the young man who tried to kill me and succeeded in murdering Marcia Williams, and the one who killed the young policewoman – unless your father did that himself.'

Liz said nothing, staring down into her empty glass and then getting up and going back to the decanter. She poured herself another larger drink.

'Who were they?'

'I don't understand.'

'Who were the hired hands? Were they ex-cons your dad happened to know – to make the conspiracy theory stick? Or just one ex-con even?'

'I'm sorry,' Liz said quietly. 'I just don't understand. Is this some kind of game?'

'You played the game as far as it would go. Both of you,' said Boyd.

'Who are you?' she said sharply.

'I'm an undercover police officer.'

'You told me you came from the prison.'

'I did.'

'Did Dad know that?'

'No. How old are you?'

'Twenty-two . . .' Liz was staring at him and Boyd wondered what she was thinking.

'As you said, you're very small – so small that you're having hormone treatment that made you ill. But despite your size you still must have had a tight squeeze in the very limited space that takes the air-conditioning round A Wing.'

Liz continued to gaze at him, her face blank.

'How did you plan the operation? How many times did you practise in that minute space? It must have been terrifying, knowing you had to arrive at exactly the right places to kill them. If you'd made one mistake you'd have landed in front of a CCTV camera.'

She still gazed at him.

'So you killed Royston, Jones and Parker. But Aidan Jones was the real target, wasn't he? Royston and Parker were simply red herrings to make the murders *look* political. How long did you both take in the planning? How did you kill these men? A little slip of a thing like you? A little slip of a thing who would be able to just squeeze yourself through the air-conditioning space and remove the already loosened grilles? And you left someone else to draw up the conspiracy theory – prison officers recruited as infiltrators – hoping to get Brand seen as the chief suspect. I didn't fail you there, did I?'

'I just don't know what you're talking about.'

'Of course you do.'

'I think you'd better go.' Liz rose to her feet.

'Do tell me where your father is.'

'If I knew I wouldn't be so worried.'

Boyd saw the fear in her eyes and for a moment he felt a stab of doubt.

'I hope you don't mind if I search the house.'

'You can't do that without getting a warrant.'

'I think you've been watching too much TV. I'm going to start my search now.'

'No need,' said Farley as he came down the stairs. He seemed to have sobered up – if he was ever drunk at all – and the hand that held the automatic was quite steady.

'I've been listening to your findings,' said Farley as he covered Boyd with the gun. 'And I can tell you that you're entirely accurate in every respect. Liz and I have been planning this operation for over a year now and we'd fine-tuned every stage.'

'How did you know she could kill?' asked Boyd, keeping him talking as a formality, as part of his training, as part of his professionalism. In fact, Boyd was suddenly hoping that Farley might be his executioner. That would be a miracle. A benign miracle.

'I underestimated you.'

'How did you know she could kill?' Boyd persisted.

'Because she loved her mother and that bastard took her away from us. At least Rhodes killed in the name of justice – just like Liz and I did.'

'Was Rhodes your inspiration?'

'He always has been my inspiration.'

'And Liz? How could you drag your daughter into all this?'

'She didn't need any dragging.'

'I can hate harder than Dad can – and I can kill. He can't,' said Liz slowly, sounding wholly matter of fact.

Was she as disturbed as Rhodes? wondered Boyd. Had her mother's murder made her as mad as he was?

'*Did* you find killing easy, Liz?' asked Boyd gently.

'Yes. Very easy. Almost a pleasure in fact. But I knew it had to be seamless – to make some kind of conspiracy seem possible – and that was enormously stressful. But I gather you bought the conspiracy theory – like everyone else did.'

'She certainly convinced you, didn't she?' Farley was almost amused.

'Once I'd killed Royston, I felt more in control,' continued Liz. 'And if I faltered for one moment I'd remember my mother. I'd remember what Jones did to her. But killing him didn't change anything, did it? I can still picture him raping and strangling her. I hadn't allowed for that.' Liz looked up at her father. 'But we're ready, aren't we?'

'Yes. I'm ready.'

Boyd knew that Farley was going to kill him and the police would put his death down to the famous conspiracy theory, which would more than cover Bill and Liz Farley's tracks. So the end was going to be tidy after all, but Boyd had no objection to that, no desire even in the face of death to hang on to a life that would only be

a series of new iden
Boyd behind once aga

But the professional
officer, was still in charge,
question. 'How did she know
that the inmates went to the toi

Farley produced a small two-w
jacket. Liz did the same from her dressing gown pocket
and they placed the radios on the low coffee table in
front of them.

'There's the evidence,' said Liz. 'And we've written a
full confession which is in the top right-hand drawer of
the little antique bureau over there.'

Boyd was confused. 'Why are you doing all this? If
you kill me no one's going to start disbelieving the
conspiracy theory. Why should they? Nothing else will
happen, of course, but that could be put down to the
conspirators' decision to close down the operation.
There would be no more strikes, nor would there be any
arrests. The case will go cold. And that will be that.'

'No,' said Liz Farley. 'I'm afraid there's been a mis-
understanding.'

Boyd stared at them. 'What kind of misunder-
standing?'

'You're quite safe,' said Farley, warmly, sympathet-
ically. 'There's nothing to worry about. Excuse me.'

With considerable precision he put the gun to his
daughter's mouth and pulled the trigger. Then he
turned it on himself.

EnLAND.

pilogue

HM Prison Aston
24 June 2001 – 1310 hours

'You should be at lunch, Mr Rhodes.'

Rhodes was in his pod, bent over his work, as Boyd and Brand came in to see him.

'You're interrupting me,' said Rhodes. 'I don't want to be interrupted.'

'I've brought you some news,' said Boyd.

'To do with history?'

'It *is* history now.'

'What is it?'

'I'm afraid Mr Farley has committed suicide.'

'That's very inconvenient,' said Rhodes. 'He still had work to do.'

'You're going to be transferred tomorrow, William,' said Brand. 'But I'm sure you will be given similar facilities at Broadmoor, although I can't guarantee another Farley.'

'What about you, Mr Taylor?' asked Rhodes. 'Can you lend me a hand?'

'Not at Broadmoor I can't. But until then . . .'

'Ah, well.' Rhodes seemed philosophic. 'I'm naturally hoping for access to a good public library. Can you guarantee that, Mr Brand?'

'I've spoken to the authorities. I gather there's an excellent library in the vicinity.'

'And someone will change my books?'

'I'm sure they will,' said Brand. 'I just can't guarantee such a devoted assistant as Bill Farley.'

'Life is unpredictable,' said Rhodes, even more philosophic now. 'Fortunately, history isn't.' He looked at Boyd. 'I've finished with the book you borrowed for me. Perhaps you would be good enough to return it tomorrow.'

'Of course,' said Boyd. 'I'd be glad to fill my time.'

Chap